The Sixth Floor

Where romance and homicide intersect

Sydney Burns Turnbull

iUniverse, Inc.
New York   Bloomington

The Sixth Floor

iUniverse books may be ordered through booksellers or by contacting:

iUniverse
1663 Liberty Drive
Bloomington, IN 47403
www.iuniverse.com
1-800-Authors (1-800-288-4677)

Because of the dynamic nature of the Internet, any Web addresses or links contained in this book may have changed since publication and may no longer be valid. The views expressed in this work are solely those of the author and do not necessarily reflect the views of the publisher, and the publisher hereby disclaims any responsibility for them.

ISBN: 978-1-4401-4763-0 (sc)
ISBN: 978-1-4401-4765-4 (dj)
ISBN: 978-1-4401-4764-7 (ebk)

Printed in the United States of America

iUniverse rev. date: 6/23/2009

In Memory of my husband

And with gratitude to my family who introduced me to Nancy Drew and gave me an insatiable appetite for the three M's Mystery, Murder, and Mayhem

ACKNOWLEDGEMENTS

My appreciation to Dr. William L. Grimes, who made the beautiful cover picture of the elevator. To retired Chief Sheriff's Deputy James Scheidler, who helped with clues. To Deputy Adkins and Huntington CSI for their knowledge and help. To David Lockwood, Attorney, who steered me through the dark water of murder indictment. To Attorney Bruce Stout and his five Paralegals, who helped me understand what my heroine did at work. To Todd Chow computer genius. To Dr. Roger Rabey, pastor of First Presbyterian Church and his wife DeeDee Rabey for their encouragement and support and to Reverend Seibel of First Presbyterian and to everyone who buys this book and helps the Alzheimer's Research Association.

Huntington, West Virginia, was founded in 1871 by Collis P. Huntington of San Francisco, California. He brought the "Iron Horse"(the C&O Railroad) east to Huntington where the operating headquarters remained until 1964.

CHAPTER 1

Driving through the Blue Ridge Mountains of Virginia was awesome, Stuart loved watching the forest blaze with autumn color while she was on her way from Columbia, South Carolina, to Huntington, West Virginia. Stuart Bennet Browning was a striking blonde with brown eyes, a slightly tilted nose and a ready smile. Her hometown was Midvale, North Carolina, but her last job had been in Columbia, South Carolina. Thinking about her home brought back summer memories of a large house with a 'wrap around' front porch that traveled almost halfway around the house and giggling girls sitting on the swing waiting for the boys to arrive. Those were fun filled days but they were part of the past, now she was taking a job with a law firm in Huntington and it started next week. She was looking forward with anticipation to her new job and her new life in Huntington. A few weeks ago she had purchased a condominium in the Park Hills area and was moving in tomorrow.

It seemed forever since breakfast so Stuart stopped for lunch in Wytheville, Virginia, at a restaurant atop the Blue Ridge Mountains. As she entered the restaurant she looked around and saw that she was surrounded by mountain tops it was as if she were standing at the top of the world.

After lunch, she was on her way once more, the colorful changing scenery made the trip seem much shorter than it was. Soon she was driving through Charleston, West Virginia, the capital of the state, it wouldn't be long before she would be seeing the signs directing her to Huntington via I-64 west.

She pulled in to the hotel about five o'clock. Her furniture wouldn't be arriving until tomorrow so she would be spending the night at the hotel. After checking in she had an early dinner in the dining room, tomorrow would be long and tiring but exciting so she went to bed early dreaming of her new job and her new home.

Her condo was perfect with two bedrooms, two baths, a kitchen and a living room with a dining area. This condominium building was different than any Stuart had ever seen. Each condo had a different floor plan but each had the same square footage. It had been left to each original owner to design his or her own floor plan and have it built. Stuart's had been designed with a small foyer that opened into a large living room with a dining area. There was a hallway on the left of the front door that led to the bedrooms and the bathrooms and the kitchen was located behind the dining area. Stuart thought this floor plan must be the best in the building and even the elevator was conveniently located close to her condo. On the entire right wall of the living room were floor to ceiling windows and a sliding glass door that all looked out on a long balcony and gave a spectacular view of the city.

Stuart met the moving van at eight a.m. at the condo building, they were moving her furniture into the building through the garage. Mr. Waxler, the condo manager, was a big plus as he watched the movers transfer the furniture onto the elevator while Stuart waited on the tenth floor for the elevator to arrive. The main elevator in the building was like no other elevator Stuart had ever seen. The doors were shining brass as was the handrail circling the cage. The walls were paneled with walnut wood and the carpet was an elegant deep red; it was a pleasurable eyeful to ride. But today the freight elevator was transporting the furniture.

Moving consumed the rest of the day but by dinner time the furniture was all in place. She was glad it was Friday it gave her the weekend to put everything away, her job started on Monday. She had been a paralegal in South Carolina, but each Firm was different and the responsibilities were different.

Stuart awoke late on Saturday morning after falling into bed exhausted on Friday. She dressed and went out for breakfast and then went shopping for groceries and cleaning supplies. When she got home she put away the groceries and began unpacking boxes.

She loved her new home and the balcony where she knew she would spend lots of time in warm weather.

There was even a swimming pool that would open again next spring. The manager, John Waxler, had been so helpful; he was a bachelor and lived on the lobby floor she would meet her new neighbors in the coming weeks. The building had twelve stories with four condos on a floor, which meant that she had a lot of neighbors to meet.

The alarm went off at seven a.m.. and Stuart struggled out of bed but was still tired from moving. She went into the kitchen and turned on the coffee so it could be perking while she took a shower; she felt better after her shower and went back into her bedroom to dress. She flipped on the television to watch / listen to the morning shows. For her first day at work she had decided to wear a tailored pants suit, the muted light brown tweed with a beige sweater enhanced her blonde hair and brown eyes. Her complexion was unusually fair and she wore very little make up; lipstick and lip gloss were all she really needed. She ran a comb through her long almost straight hair, parted it on the side and some short strands fell forward making a half bang. After adding gold hoop earrings she put on her gold wristwatch and was ready for work. She grabbed a cup of coffee and some toast with jelly but the fruit would have to wait. Stuart picked up her brown shoulder bag and after locking the condo door headed for the elevator. The brass doors opened almost immediately and she stepped inside, she pushed the button for the garage and stepped back and almost into a young girl standing there, "I'm sorry! I didn't see you." Stuart apologized.

"That's okay." answered the girl.

"My name's Stuart Browning and I live in ten-o one"

"My name's Jenny." the girl replied.

"Is that short for Jennifer?"

"No, it's just Jenny." The elevator stopped at the garage and Stuart got out turning around to see if Jenny were coming. "I'm not getting off, I was on my way up when the elevator stopped at your floor," explained Jenny. The doors closed and Stuart walked to her car. Her first meeting with one of her new neighbors, the girl in the elevator named Jenny.

Stuart walked into the offices of Hunter, Lycans, Dobbs and McCarthy where she was greeted by Mary Wilson the receptionist, she was five minutes early so that made a statement about her punctuality. She walked back to the office assigned to her and hung up her coat and put away her shoulder bag. Her intercom sounded and it was Robert Dobbs' secretary asking her to come to Mr. Dobbs' office. Stuart just walked across the hall and checked in with his secretary who sent her right in to see him. Robert stood up and said "Welcome to the Firm." Stuart thanked him and asked, "Where do I start?"

"I have some real estate work that needs title searching so I thought you could do that and familiarize yourself with the courthouse."

"Fine, I'll leave right away".

On the top of the courthouse sat a large gold dome, and differing from other courthouses in cities this size it had a lush green lawn surrounding it. There were a number of handsome old buildings in the downtown area, one was the Keith Albee Theatre on Fourth Avenue, built in the '30s and full of glitter and glamour where famous entertainers and actors once 'trod the boards'. Now it was home to the Performing Arts of Marshall University. Huntington had a lot to show off including the Huntington Museum of Art which had the distinction of being the only Museum between Cincinnati, Ohio and Richmond, Virginia.

CHAPTER 2

As she was driving home Stuart's thoughts returned to Jenny, she wondered about her parents and which condo they owned. She pulled into her parking space in the garage and got out. Mr. Waxler was in the garage checking his car when he saw Stuart, he smiled and asked how her first day at work had gone. "It went really well," answered Stuart, "I spent most of the day in the courthouse but before I came home I drove down by Riverfront Park and sneaked a peek where the flood gate was open. That's a wonderful place for a park, right on the bank of the mighty Ohio River, I understand that the Huntington Symphony Orchestra gives concerts there in the summer."

"Yes, it's great there in the summer." said Mr. Waxler.

"Say, Mr. Waxler, I met one of my neighbors on the elevator this morning."

"Who did you meet?"

"I met a pretty but shy teenager named Jenny".

"There's no one here by that name and we don't have any teenagers in the building, she must have been visiting." commented Mr. Waxler.

"She had long strawberry blond hair and the loveliest green eyes and she was wearing lime colored "low-slung" jeans and a white sweater that almost met the jeans but not quite. She was also wearing a pewter 'peace symbol' on a narrow leather strap, reminiscent of the 60's."

"I haven't seen any one fitting that description but then I don't see everyone who visits here." said Mr. Waxler.

Stuart headed for the elevator and pushed the button, she got off on the tenth floor and fumbled for the key in her shoulder bag. As the door opened she gazed into her living room and thought how lucky she was. She enjoyed her new home and after today she knew she would be happy in her new job too.

Stuart hung up her pants suit and put on an exercise suit to go jogging in the park, Ritter Park. The park began across the street from the condo building, it was beautiful and sat in the middle of a lovely residential area. It had much to offer, a great walking / running track, a gorgeous rose garden, a picnic area, a well manicured lawn and in the middle of it all, a large fountain overflowing with clear sparkling water. In the cool autumn weather jogging was a perfect way to relax and get some exercise at the same time.

On the way home Stuart stopped at the drugstore and bought a Hershey bar, she loved chocolate. She waited until she was inside the building and had rung for the elevator before she unwrapped it. The elevator slipped down and the doors opened, Stuart stepped inside and pushed the button for her floor; she stepped back and almost into Jenny again. This gave her a start and she said, "Again I didn't see you, how are you?" Jenny replied that she was fine.

"I told Mr. Waxler that I had met you this morning but he said he didn't know you, that you were probably visiting someone here." Stuart began.

"Is that a Hershey bar you're eating?" asked Jenny "that used to be my favorite candy."

"Yes, it's my favorite too, sorry I don't have another one to offer you." replied Stuart. The elevator stopped on ten and as Stuart got off she said "Bye." and the door closed. Stuart was beginning to have a different sort of feeling about Jenny, not eerie or frightening, just different. The back of her neck felt funny when she was around her. She must talk to her longer the next time they met, this was all very curious.

Stuart took a shower and put on her robe, it was a cool evening but she opened the sliding glass door to the balcony and stepped outside for a minute. She loved looking at the stars and the lights at night made the city look mysterious and unknown. Stuart wondered what went on behind the lights in the houses, they were all different and the people who lived in them were too. A cool breeze put a chill in the air so she came back inside and closed the glass door.

She put on a CD by a new singer named Michael Buble and sat down in her most comfortable chair to listen. As she sat listening to the music she wondered if she had really made the right choice in coming to live in Huntington. Her mother had said she should 'spread her wings' because she could always come home. She'd had a nice life in Columbia, made a lot of friends and had an active social life. That reminded her of Chuck, she had met him shortly after moving to Columbia, he was so much fun, he was good-looking, clever, and had a great out-going personality. He had introduced her to a group that planned something to do almost every weekend. They had gone dancing at different clubs, gone on picnics in the mountains, and on some Saturdays had gone to Litchfield Beach to lie on the sand and watch the ocean. Chuck was an aide to the governor, whose office was in Columbia, and he often traveled with the governor around the state. Stuart and Chuck had dated almost a year when he asked her to marry him. He had taken a job in Washington with one of South Carolina's senators and wanted Stuart to marry him and move to Washington with him. It sounded terribly exciting, living in Washington and being so close to the seat of world power but there was "a fly in the ointment "…she wasn't in love with Chuck. She enjoyed being with him but for the rest of her life? In the end she had to say no and she had hated hurting him. That was really why she had moved to Huntington, she needed to get away from everything that Columbia had meant to her.

She began to see that life was full of doorways. Each door led you into a different life. If you wanted to see what was on the other side you walked thru the door. If you liked where you were you left the door unopened. She had been ready for the next door so when the door appeared with "Huntington" written on it she had walked through anxiously waiting to see what was on the other side. She had found Jenny on the other side and that was a strange meeting, why did the elevator go down if Jenny had already pushed the up button? Obviously Jenny was going up or she would have gotten off before the tenth floor. Elevators are run by computers and when they are programmed to go up then they continue to go up until they reach the desired floor. What was going on? Tonight she obviously did not want to talk about why she was in the building instead she changed the subject to Stuart's candy bar.

CHAPTER 3

He used his key and opened the door on the deck and entered the building; the deck was beside the pool but nobody was out there this time of year. Quickly he stepped inside and disappeared into the darkened room. He thought about taking the elevator to the sixth floor but decided to walk, the noise of the elevator might arouse people and he didn't want anyone to have memories about tonight. Very carefully he opened the door on the sixth floor while he glanced up and down the corridor. Seeing no one and hearing nothing he walked to the door of 603. He shoved his credit card in between the door lock and the door facing, the lock clicked once and the door was open. Why did people keep buying locks that could be opened so easily?

Once inside he put on rubber gloves, he'd seen enough TV to know all about leaving fingerprints. The lights shouldn't be turned on so he used his flashlight to find the closet where the coins were hidden. Mrs. Martin had been discussing the coins over the phone when he overheard her say that they were probably worth $10,000 now. The coins were kept in a large metal box guarded only by a Yale lock. Searching for the box took a few minutes, it was on the floor under a wooden box that was turned upside down and served as a shelf for shoes. He pulled the box out into the middle of the closet and gave one hard swipe at the lock with a wrench and it fell away; he opened the box and found a smaller box containing the coins; it wasn't as heavy as he expected, it could be carried easily. Now walking toward the foyer he saw the front door open and the overhead lights flash on, there stood Mrs. Martin looking straight at him screaming, "You! What are you doing in my condominium!"

"I can explain" replied the man as he walked toward her, another quick swipe with the wrench and Mrs. Martin lay on the floor, silent. He made a fast exit, closed the door and hid behind an ornamental tree in the corridor. As soon as he decided that no one had heard the commotion he entered the stairwell once again.

While it was still dark he entered his home. He hid the coins in the laundry basket and piled the dirty clothes on top. Then he sat down and thought about the other time; it had been a female that time too, the girl had caught him cheating and was going to report him to the school principal. He had followed her hoping to talk her out of it but she wouldn't listen. They came to the top of the stairs leading down to the first floor and all he'd had to do was give her a little nudge and down the stairs she fell, breaking her neck along the way. It was a shame too, she had had such beautiful red hair.

Everyone thought she had tripped and fallen, no one thought he'd had anything to do with it, he even went to the funeral. She had caused her own death just like Mrs. Martin, they shouldn't have threatened him it was their fault that they had died.

CHAPTER 4

Stuart awoke before the alarm went off. She had been at the law firm almost a month now and was becoming adjusted to the routine. She dressed, ate her breakfast of coffee, toast, and fruit and was ready for work. She rang for the elevator and when it arrived she looked carefully for Jenny before she stepped in, but no Jenny appeared. She hadn't seen her for several days.

It was after lunch when Stuart received a call from Mr. Waxler shocking her beyond belief.

"Mrs. Martin on the sixth floor was murdered last night!"

Stuart drew in her breath sharply and gasped, "What?"

Mr. Waxler continued "The police are here now and want to see everyone in the building as soon as people get home from work."

"Should I come home now?" questioned Stuart.

"No, the police and CSI (Crime Scene Investigators) are here now but they don't need to see you all until later."

"What happened?"

"As near as can be determined she was killed sometime last night, Mr. Martin came home today and found her. They had been away together. He had attended a business meeting. She came home alone last evening because she had a dental appointment this morning. Right now that's all I know"

"I'll be home around five" responded Stuart.

"Go to the meeting room on the lobby floor when you get here" instructed Mr. Waxler before he hung up. Stuart couldn't concentrate on work after this awful news. She had thought she would be safe in a condo. What could have happened? She didn't think she could wait until five o'clock to find out.

The afternoon dragged by but it was finally time to leave. Stuart got in her car and was home in just a few minutes. She parked in the garage and took the elevator to the lobby, when she got off Mr. Waxler was standing in the hallway talking to a uniformed policeman. There was another policeman standing by the front entrance. Mr. Waxler spoke and then opened the door to the meeting room and motioned her inside. He introduced Stuart to the man standing in the middle of the room.

"This is Chief Detective Moore" he explained and then turned to the detective and said," This is Miss Browning who lives in ten o one." As Stuart extended her hand to Detective Moore she was staring into the bluest eyes she had ever seen and the detective was looking at a beautiful young woman in a beige pants suit. Stuart quickly looked away as detective Moore told her that he had to interview everyone in the building. He was starting with the first floor owners. Since she lived on the tenth floor it would be some time before he got to her so she decided to go on up to her condo and wait.

She took the elevator to the tenth floor, got off and went inside to wait. She fixed a sandwich and a salad and sat down to watch the evening news. The murder had made the six o'clock news but no details were available. Finally Stuart decided to go back down to the lobby and see if Detective Moore were ready to interview her. When the elevator arrived at the lobby Stuart saw the door was open to the meeting room and a couple was walking out. What a way to meet your new neighbors! Detective Moore invited Stuart inside and closed the door. They sat down at a table and he began by telling her that his name was David. She replied that hers was Stuart. The questioning didn't last long because she didn't know anything and was shocked by the murder. She told him that she'd only lived here about a month and hadn't heard anything unusual last night.

"What time did it happen?" she asked him. He told her that the CSI unit was still in the condo working but should be finished any time and we wouldn't know anything until they finished. David asked where she worked and what she did. She replied "I work at Hunter, Lycans, Dobbs and McCarthy as a paralegal or legal assistant."

"Where did you go to school?"

"I graduated from Marshall and I liked the time I spent in Huntington so well that I came back. How about you?"

"Well, I graduated from Marshall, too, in Criminal Justice and went to work for the Police Department." he replied.

Stuart knew there were other people waiting to be interviewed so she stood and told David that if he needed anything more from her she would be glad to help in any way that she could. David answered "There may be more questions after the CSI investigation is completed."

"Then you're in charge of the investigation?" Stuart asked.

"Yes, it's my case but I must add that it's not my first murder case".

"I hope you solve this quickly, it makes me more than a little apprehensive living where a murder took place last night!" Stuart added. David told her that she was safe here, not to worry and then told her good evening.

CHAPTER 5

Stuart rang for the elevator and was engrossed in thoughts of the murder when it arrived. She stepped inside and there stood Jenny in her lime colored jeans.

"Hey "Stuart said, "where have you been?"

"Just around," Jenny answered.

"You know about the murder in 603?"

"Yes, it's terrible, I didn't think such a thing could happen here." Stuart decided to push Jenny just a little and asked, "You don't live here, do you?"

"No, I just visit from time to time."

Stuart continued "I don't suppose that you'll be questioned by the police since you don't live here, but the detective in charge of the case is dead attractive."

"That's a strange way to describe a man in charge of a murder case." replied Jenny.

"I guess it is but it's true, you'll see." continued Stuart. The elevator stopped on the lobby floor and Mr. Waxler got on. They spoke and Stuart turned around to introduce Jenny but Jenny wasn't there! Had she gotten off in the lobby and Stuart hadn't seen her?

By now the elevator was in the garage and the doors were opening. Mr. Waxler went to his car after telling Stuart he had some errands to do and would see her later.

Driving to work Stuart wondered some more about Jenny. What did she really know about the murder? Was she your average teenager or someone quite different? Did she actually get off the elevator or did she just vanish?

Once more after lunch Stuart was called to the phone. It was Mr. Waxler again, " Miss Browning, the police want everyone in the building to be finger printed so sometime today go to the police station and have it done."

"Anytime during the day?" questioned Stuart.

"Yes, whenever you have time" answered Mr. Waxler.

"Thank you" replied Stuart as she hung up. Well, she thought, this was just like in the movies. She hardly believed it was anyone in the building but she guessed the police had to start somewhere, besides maybe she would get to see that good -looking detective again.

Everyone in the law firm wanted to know all about the murder but Stuart didn't have much to tell. Now she could tell them about being finger printed. She took some time and drove to the police station. She walked in and told the desk sergeant who she was and why she was here. It didn't take long to get her prints taken but she didn't see her "favorite" detective any place around. She got back to the office and finished typing some depositions she had taken for Mr. Dobbs earlier in the day.. As she was leaving Mr. Dobbs stopped her saying "You know if you need a lawyer for anything or to answer any questions for you , call me day or night."

"Thank you" answered Stuart "but I hope I won't need to".

When Stuart arrived at the condo she went straight to Mr. Waxler's apartment and rang his doorbell. He answered the door, greeted Stuart with a smile and asked, "What can I do for you?"

"Has everyone been fingerprinted?"

"As far as I know, yes." answered Mr. Waxler.

"Any new evidence or leads?" asked Stuart.

"If there is I haven't heard about it" replied Mr. Waxler.

"Well, thanks, if you hear anything would you please let me know?"

"Certainly, but don't be afraid, I'm taking extra precaution to be sure everyone will be safe," Waxler informed her.

Stuart took the elevator to the tenth floor and got off before she remembered that she hadn't seen Jenny on the elevator. The last time she had seen Jenny was when Mr. Waxler got on the elevator this morning. She couldn't have gotten off without Stuart seeing her and she really couldn't have disappeared or could she?

CHAPTER 6

Chief of police Connally called David to his office to discuss the Martin case. "Just what do we know about the murder?" questioned the chief.

"The CSI unit found that the murderer was probably left handed and that Mrs. Martin died immediately. They also found two sets if fingerprints that don't belong to the Martins. I asked all the other residents in the building to be finger printed and they were." answered David.

"Did the fingerprints match any of the residents?"

"No, with the exception of the condo manager, Mr. Waxler, who of course has been in all the condos at one time or another." replied the detective.

"Do we have a motive? Did the Martins get along?" asked the chief.

"$10,000 in coins is missing so that could be the motive but no one seems to know much about the private life of the Martins." said David.

"How was she killed?"

"The proverbial blunt instrument." responded David.

"Did CSI determine the time of death?"

"Yes," answered David, "sometime between 11 pm and 1 am. Mr. and Mrs. Martin had been out of town for several days while Mr. Martin attended a business meeting. She came home early because she had a dental appointment".

"Did you say she flew home?" inquired the chief.

"Yes, her plane arrived at Tri State airport at ten and she took a cab home. I've talked to the cabbie and he remembers arriving at the condo at about ten forty five p.m." David continued, "I think someone was waiting for her or she surprised a burglar stealing the coins."

"Do a little more digging into the Martin's past and into their relationship with the other owners", ordered the chief.

"This case may be harder than it first appeared. Mr. Martin's alibi seems rock solid after questioning the hotel and the airlines, so we have to find another path to follow." answered David as he went back to his office. He called Mr.Waxler and made an appointment to see him before dinner, at the condo.

Mr. Waxler was waiting when David pulled up to the condo building. They went into Mr. Waxler's apartment instead of the condo meeting room. Mr. Waxler closed the door and showed David to a chair. "Can I fix you something to drink?" Mr. Waxler asked.

"No, thank you," answered David as he smiled "I'm still technically on duty. What can you tell me about the Martins? Did they get along well and what was their relationship with the other residents?"

"Well, they were nice people but kept to themselves mostly I think everyone liked them but didn't know them very well. They were always thoughtful of me and so appreciative of anything I did for them." responded Mr. Waxler.

"Did they have many visitors? Did they entertain people who didn't live in the building?" questioned David.

"I can't really answer that, I know they didn't have large parties or entertain a lot, I think they weren't socially inclined."

"There are some fingerprints in their condo that can't be identified and I'm wondering who they belong to," said David.

"Well," offered Mr. Waxler, "we do have workmen here several times a year doing work for the owners. Maybe the Martins had some work done recently."

"I'll ask Mr. Martin about that and by the way, are you right or left handed?" inquired David.

"I'm left handed" replied Mr. Waxler. David stood up and thanked Mr. Waxler for his time and left. Stuart was just stepping off the elevator when David left Mr. Waxler's apartment. "Good evening, detective" said Stuart smiling. "Good evening Miss Browning how are you?"

"I'm fine, thank you, but I'd be a lot finer if you would hurry and solve this case!" answered Stuart.

"I'm doing my best" said David with a smile.

"Seriously, do you have any new information?" asked Stuart.

"No, not yet but the night is young!" responded David facetiously as Stuart walked to the front door with him. She retrieved her mail from her box at the front entrance, they said goodnight and he left and she walked back to the elevator. She pushed the button and looked through her mail while the elevator was coming down. The door opened, she stepped in and there stood Jenny. "Well, where did you disappear to this morning, I was going to introduce you to Mr. Waxler?"

"Oh, I slipped off the elevator while he was getting on," said Jenny.

"You just missed detective Moore, he was here to see Mr. Waxler" Stuart informed her.

"He doesn't think Mr. Waxler had anything to do with the murder, does he?" asked Jenny.

"I'm sure not, he probably just wanted more information about the people who live here." By this time they had arrived at the tenth floor and the door opened. "Why don't you come in and visit with me awhile?" asked Stuart.

"I'd like to but I can't," answered Jenny. The elevator door closed and Jenny was gone again. Stuart didn't believe Jenny's story about getting off the elevator into the lobby this morning. She was sincere enough when she told Stuart but Stuart knew that getting off was impossible. She hadn't seen her, Mr. Waxler hadn't seen her, so the only other explanation was that she had disappeared. That was impossible, too. She either existed only in Stuart's mind or she was a ghost, neither of these explanations pleased or satisfied Stuart. This was as eerie as Mrs., Martin's murder.

CHAPTER 7

David went to the chief's office again to discuss the murder. The case seemed to be stuck in low gear.

"Chief" said David "I'm having no luck finding a suspect except for Waxler, the manager, he has keys to all the condos plus keys to all the outside doors and he's left handed and knew about the coins."

"That's more evidence than you have against anyone else and you haven't found any new leads" answered Chief Connally.

"I just can't believe that Waxler would be that obvious, he knows he would be the prime suspect if anyone were killed or robbed in the condo building, since he has all the keys." continued David.

"Why don't you question that girl you think is so attractive? sometimes people who are new to the surroundings can spot things and feel things that the others can't because of their familiarity with the scene," prompted the chief, "besides it's not a bad idea to make friends with her, we could use an inside eye and ear on this case, maybe we'll learn something useful, I know you'll find this hard to take but force yourself," said the chief with a half smile. He did so enjoy needling his chief detective, who was his best and most favorite detective on the force. But then all the men on the force liked David, he was a real man's man. "I'll just do that," said David as he went back to his office and dialed Stuart's number at work.

"This is Stuart Browning," answered Stuart.

"This is David Moore and I was wondering if you would have dinner with me this evening and discuss the case a bit? "

"Why, yes, just tell me where and when." replied Stuart.

"I'll pick you up around seven." answered David.

"Sounds fine, I'll see you then." said Stuart as she hung up the phone. She thought about David and wondered what he could gain from talking to her when she didn't know anything.

She pulled into the garage and parked her car. She was still thinking about her dinner date when she got on the elevator. The doors closed and Jenny said "hello". Stuart was surprised to see her and quickly decided that now was the time to get some answers so she pulled out the "stop" button and the elevator stopped. She turned to Jenny and questioned "Are you a figment of my imagination or are you real?"

Jenny just looked at her for a long minute before she answered, "I'm not really either one."

"What do you mean?" asked Stuart.

After a long pause and with a stutter Jenny replied.

"I'm a...... I'm a ghost."

"You're what?" exclaimed Stuart.

"I'm a ghost," repeated Jenny.

"There's no such thing!" Stuart answered, trying to sound positive and unafraid.

Silence was the only reply she got.

"Well, how did you get to be a ghost?"

"I don't remember anymore than you remember being born, I live in a different dimension in time and space." Again Stuart questioned her, "Why am I the only one who sees you?"

"I don't know that either, you're the first one who has ever been able to see me."

"What are you doing in the elevator?"

"An elevator is a perfect place for me, I'm suspended between two worlds and the elevator is suspended between floors," replied Jenny "and besides, this elevator is beautiful."

"Why are you here now when Mrs. Martin has just been murdered?" demanded Stuart.

"I'm looking for some answers and since you can see me I was hoping you would help me."

"How in the world could I help a ghost, if you are a ghost?"

"You can do things that I can't."

"This is too much, I'm getting off this elevator!" exclaimed Stuart as she pushed the elevator button in and it continued its way to the tenth floor.

She was in a trance-like state as she left the elevator and stood in front of her door. She couldn't believe what had just happened. This is more than I really wanted to know thought Stuart. I didn't dream her answer would be such a shock. Could I have imagined it all? She stood in the middle of her living room trying to make sense of Jenny when all of a sudden she had to change mental gears. David was due and she barely had time to freshen her makeup and comb her hair.

The buzzer sounded, Stuart answered it and told David to come on up. She was standing in her open doorway when the elevator came to a stop and David got off.

"Good evening." said David as he approached her.

"Come in while I get my jacket and purse." answered Stuart.

David looked around and whistled softly. "What a super condo and what an amazing view of the city!"

"Yes, I like it here and enjoy my balcony a lot." offered Stuart "at least I did until the murder."

"May I step outside a minute?" asked David. "Your view is just perfect and as for the murder, don't worry we'll get whoever did this."

"I'm almost afraid to go out there now, someone could slip inside while I'm outside and then murder me when I come back in." Stuart answered and left to get her things.

"Where are we going to dinner?" she asked as she stepped back onto the balcony beside him.

"I thought the Iron Horse Inn, it's quiet so we can talk and the food is good."

"Sounds nice." answered Stuart.

The Iron Horse Inn was a restaurant tucked away among the houses in an older residential area. The streets surrounding it were red brick and the street light in front was an old fashioned lantern hung on a tall post. It was electric, of course, but it was in keeping with the personality of the neighborhood.

The minute they stepped into the elevator Stuart's thoughts raced back to Jenny. Wonder what David would think if she told him about her conversation with Jenny? She couldn't of course, he would think she was a "card short of a full deck." David drove a sleek black Chevrolet Impala with a stick shift and as he opened the door Stuart noticed how neat and clean it was. This wasn't a city car of course, it was his own personal car, the detective drove a good looking automobile. The Iron Horse wasn't too far away so they arrived in a matter of minutes, David parked the car and they walked to the door, once inside the hostess showed them to a booth. The Iron Horse had a few booths but more tables and a large wood-burning fireplace. It was an attractive restaurant, decorated like an English tavern with a lot of pewter around. The waitress came to take their drink orders and Stuart ordered a glass of white wine while David ordered a glass of red wine. After their drinks arrived they settled in comfortably and began to play 'twenty questions'.

"Tell me about yourself, your family, where you're from and why you decided to live in Huntington" quizzed David.

"Well" began Stuart, "I'm from a small town in North Carolina where my father is a dentist and my mother stays busy with her church work and various charitable endeavors. I have a brother, Johnny, who's a couple of years older and is doing his residency in Family Practice. Why did I come to Huntington? I visited several colleges and my grades allowed me to pick and choose where I would go. Marshall University was about the right size, not too large, and I loved the small town atmosphere of Huntington. After I graduated I got a job in Columbia, South Carolina with a large law firm. While Columbia is a beautiful city and the Spring Lake Country Club is really neat, I found it too large for me. Huntington was more the size city that I liked. Is that enough background for you, detective?" teased Stuart. "Now it's your turn."

"I'm from a small town, too, in Kentucky. A town named Whitesville. Dad is a lawyer and my mother is the local librarian. I'm an only child and I came to Marshall on a golf scholarship. After I graduated I got a job with the Huntington Police Department and I'm still trying to decide if I want to go on to law school. Detective work is so much more interesting than legal work. Having always liked mysteries I'm now getting to help solve them and put the bad guys away."

The waitress arrived just then with their menus. They studied the choices and both decided on Beef

Stroganoff and garden salads with coffee later. After the waitress left Stuart asked about the case and if there were any new leads.

"No, we seem to be just treading water, have you heard anything from the other owners?" asked David.

"I'm so new to the building that I don't really know anyone yet, but I did overhear two of the women, as they were getting off the elevator, say something about Mr. Martin and a girl in his office but it just sounded like gossip to me." related Stuart.

"His alibi is iron clad for the night his wife was murdered but of course he could have had someone else do it." reflected David.

"I hate to think I have a neighbor who could have had his wife murdered ! but stranger things have happened and if there were another woman involved, who knows what could have happened." said Stuart.

"What do you think of Mr. Waxler?" asked David.

"He's been very helpful to me and seems like a genuinely nice man. You surely don't think he could be involved do you?" questioned Stuart.

"I don't like to think so but everyone is under suspicion," answered David.

"Surely not me!" exclaimed Stuart.

"No, not really," he responded, "but you could have seen something or heard something or formed an opinion about something that could help with the case. You do know that $10,000 in rare coins is missing from the condo?"

"No, I hadn't heard that, the coins could be the motive and she surprised a burglar." ventured Stuart.

"Or else the husband made it look like burglary so he wouldn't be suspected." offered David, "and of course Mr. Waxler had a key to the condo."

"You've narrowed it down to two suspects?" asked Stuart.

"For right now, yes, but there are some other things I need to look into, there are some fingerprints that can't be identified and they don't belong to any of the other owners in the building."

Their dinner arrived and put an end to any more talk of the murder. The stroganoff was exceptional and the conversation became more pleasant again. Their coffee arrived after dinner and they began to discuss the latest movie, which they had both seen and both agreed was disappointing.

David paid the check and they walked outside to the car. When they arrived back at the condo David helped her out of the car and stood while she unlocked the door to the building. Then he followed her inside and up to her condo.

"I would invite you in for coffee but we've already had our coffee" said Stuart jokingly, "but thank you for a most interesting evening and a delicious dinner and do keep me updated on your progress."

"Thank you for being such an interesting dinner companion and allowing me a very pleasant evening,

I will keep you informed and if you hear anything let me know." said David as he smiled and turned to leave.

Stuart closed the door and leaned back against it thinking about David and how much she had enjoyed the evening. She hoped there were more to come, maybe she didn't want the murder solved so quickly after all. She put on a CD and sat down to listen. Michael Buble was singing "Witchcraft," another Sinatra favorite, when suddenly she wasn't hearing "Witchcraft" anymore. Her head was spinning with thoughts of Jenny, the ghost!

CHAPTER 8

David went over his facts concerning the murder and arranged a meeting with Mr. Martin. They decided to meet at Martin's office, he was a C.P.A. and his office was downtown.

David walked into the offices of Martin C.P.A. Inc. and spoke to the receptionist. She directed him to Mr. Martin's office. "Well, detective, do you have anything new to tell me about my wife's murder?"

"I'm afraid not, sir" answered David, "I'm here hoping that you can give me some new information. You know that we have found two sets of fingerprints in your condo that we can't identify."

"Yes, your chief told me about them."

"I'm hoping you can remember who might have been in your condo recently, friends, relatives or workmen, so we can tie up that loose end" said David. Mr .Martin thought a minute and then answered "We had a new hot water tank installed about two weeks ago. It could have been the plumbers who left the prints. There were two men but I've dealt with this company for years and I'm sure they had nothing to do with my wife's murder".

"What is the name of the plumbing company and the names of the two men?" asked David.

"The company is Sims and Sims and the two men are Don and Harry." replied Mr. Martin.

"I'll ask them if they will consent to being fingerprinted and maybe that will solve one of our problems" said David as he stood to leave. "If you remember anything more, no matter how insignificant, please call me." continued David as he walked to the door.

David's next stop was Sims and Sims. He parked his car on their lot and walked to the front door. When he got inside he asked to see the manager. "The manager's not here" the receptionist informed him. "May I help you?"

"I'd like to speak to Don and Harry who work here." continued David as he showed her his badge.

"They're not in any trouble are they?" exclaimed the receptionist.

"Oh, no, I just wanted to question them about a job they did two or three weeks ago".

"Don's here but Harry's out on a call, shall I get Don for you?"

"Yes, please" replied David.

A tall man about forty years old came walking up and told David that his name was Don. "Mr. Martin who lives in the Park Hills condominiums told me that you and Harry replaced a hot water tank in his condo two or three weeks ago."

"That's right we did, there's nothing wrong is there?" answered Don.

"I'm sure you've read in the newspaper about Mrs. Martin's murder."

"Yes, of course, I'm sorry. She was a nice lady."

"I'm the detective in charge of the case and I want to ask you and Harry if you would mind having your prints taken at the station?" asked David.

"Harry isn't here but I wouldn't mind at all, just tell me when."

"The sooner the better, and could you ask Harry too? You both could come together. There are some unidentified prints at the condo and since you were recently there on a job I'm hoping they are yours and then we can close that door." informed David.

Don answered that they would be happy to comply and would have their prints made as soon as possible.

David drove back to the Police Station and went in to see Chief Connally.

"Well, chief, I've just spoken to one of the two plumbers who were at the Martin's condo to replace a hot water tank a couple of weeks ago. Maybe their finger prints will turn out to be the unidentified ones."

"I can't make up my mind whether this is an outside or an inside job" said the chief, "There's no evidence of a break-in, either into the building or into the Martin's condo."

"I know," said David "neither of the Martins seem to have any enemies and with no evidence supporting a break-in, our only suspect thus far is Waxler."

"Did you check out those rumors about Martin having a girlfriend?" asked Chief Connally.

"I have an appointment this afternoon to interview everyone in Martin's office. It's been my experience that in interviewing women or men that work together there's always one that's eager to talk. I'm hoping I can find that one today and come up with something useful." answered David.

"Well, get back to me." replied the chief.

CHAPTER 9

David entered Mr. Martin's office, spoke to the receptionist and asked to see Mr. Martin. "He's expecting you, detective, go right in." David walked into the office and spoke to Mr. Martin.

"Where would you like me to conduct the interviews?"

"I think you could use the conference room. That would be the easiest." directed Mr. Martin.

"Tell your receptionist to send them in, one at a time, starting with your newest junior partner, Rosemary Howard. I'll go on into the conference room and wait." The conference room had a large table, surrounded by chairs, in the middle of the room. This was perfect, David sat down to wait. The door opened and there stood a good looking brunette, dressed 'fit to kill' and introduced herself as Rosemary Howard. David stood and then asked her to sit down. "We're interviewing everyone who knew the Martins so that includes their business associates. We're hoping that maybe somebody can shed some light on this murder investigation." began David. "Do you know of anyone who disliked Mr. Martin or held a grudge against the Firm?"

"No" said Rosemary," just the opposite, this Firm has a very good reputation for contented clients and competent accountants. That's why I wanted to work here and was so pleased that I was hired."

"How long have you been here?" asked David.

"Almost two years" replied Rosemary.

"And there's never been a problem with a client or anyone working here?" questioned David.

"No, it's a great place to work."

"Well, thank you for your time, Miss Howard " said David. "If you remember anything or if anything out of the ordinary happens let us know."

"Oh, I will, detective, you can be sure." answered Rosemary with a flirtatious smile. David sat down again to wait for the next woman. The door opened and another woman appeared; this one was about sixty, graying a little and carrying a few pounds too many. "I'm Martha Ratliff and I'm Mr. Martin's secretary." she said.

"I'm detective David Moore and I promise to not take much of your time, how long have you worked for Mr. Martin?"

"Oh, I've been with Mr. Martin from the beginning of the Firm, about twenty five years." replied Martha.

"Well then, you know as much about the Firm as he does, do you know of anyone who could have a grudge against the Firm or Mr. Martin?"

"Oh no, Mr. Martin is a lovely gentleman and we have nothing but satisfied clients."

"Do you know if any of the employees could be dissatisfied?" asked David.

"Not with Mr. Martin" Martha replied.

"What does that mean?" questioned David.

"We all got along fine until *she* came."

"Who is *she*?"

"Miss Howard with her nose pointed at the ceiling."

"So she's a snob, has Mr. Martin noticed this trait?"

"Not hardly, butter would melt in her mouth when he's around."

"Do the others feel as you do?"

"Yes, she's only nice to Mr. Martin and I suspect there are times when she's more than nice to him!"

"Is she married?" asked David.

"No, but she'd like to be." answered Martha.

"Does Mr. Martin return her admiration?"

"Now Detective, you know as well as I do that you men can only stand so much 'admiration'........"

"Miss Ratliff, are you suggesting that Mr. Martin is having an affair with Miss Howard?"

"No, no, I'm not suggesting anything, I just wouldn't be surprised at anything" answered Martha.

"But you don't know of anyone here who carries a grudge against Mr. Martin?" questioned David.

"No indeed, everyone is very fond of Mr. Martin and is upset about Mrs. Martin and would like to help in any way that we could."

"Well, thank you for your time, Miss Ratliff and if you remember anything pertinent to any problems the Firm might have please let me know".

"Oh, I will detective, I hope you catch whoever did this awful thing, Mrs. Martin was a darling lady." David sat thinking after she left, I've found my 'eager to talk' so I don't need to do any more interviews but that would look suspicious. I'll have to interview the other two women. He met with the two women and they talked but they didn't know anything. He thanked them for their time and left.

Chief Connally was busy talking with CSI when David got back to Headquarters. He went into the chief's office to wait. Shortly thereafter the chief returned "Well did you learn anything?"

"Yes, I think I did, as I had hoped I found a talkative employee. One who has been with the Firm since it's beginning."

"Is Martin having an affair?"

"This secretary of Martin's suggests that he is but she's not positive." answered David.

"What do you think?" asked Connally.

"I interviewed the lady in question and she's good looking but the only way to be sure is to shadow her a few days and see."

"I don't have a man I can spare right now" replied the chief.

"What about a woman? That new gal who partners with Detective Harkins?" offered David, "besides a woman wouldn't look as suspicious as a man."

"Well," answered Connally" I'll call her in and see about it".

Detective Ann Derrick walked into the chief's office and asked "You want to see me chief?"

"Yes, detective, I'm wondering if you could do a little spy job?"

"Exactly what do you want me to do?"

"It concerns the Martin case. We have reason to believe that Martin is having an affair with a woman in his office" explained Connally.

"You think he may have killed his wife for this other woman? I thought his alibi checked out".

"No, we don't think he did it but he could have hired someone, wouldn't be the first time".

"Then I'm to check on her comings and goings?" asked Detective Derrick.

"Yes," answered Connally "for a few days so we can determine if he's having an affair."

"Then I'll get right on it, where is her office and where does she live?" Ann inquired.

"You can get all that from Chief Detective Moore" replied Connally.

This was Ann's first time following a "person of interest". She went home to change clothes first so she would look like someone she wasn't. She found the right building and parked a half a block from Martin's office and waited for Rosemary Howard to leave for the day. At quarter past five Miss Howard walked out and Detective Derrick watched her walk to the parking garage. When she drove out the exit Detective Derrick pulled out too, putting two cars between them. She followed Rosemary home and again parked a half a block away. From this vantage point she could see clearly if Mr. Martin came to see Rosemary. Ann munched on a sandwich and drank a cup of coffee while she waited. Finally after midnight and the lights in Howard's apartment were off and her car hadn't moved, Ann left.

Early the next morning Ann Derrick came to Connally's office to report.

"See anything interesting last night?" asked the chief.

"Not a thing" answered Ann "she went straight home and later went to bed so I left shortly after midnight."

"Well try again tonight, detective, maybe something will happen, after all its Saturday night." joked Connally.

Ann followed Rosemary all day but didn't see anything interesting, just groceries, dry cleaners, and a trip to the drug store. At about 5:30 Rosemary got in her car and left again. Ann followed her across the Ohio river and into Ohio ---- now it was getting interesting. She drove to a relatively new housing development and parked in the underground garage of a multi-unit apartment building. Ann drove on past the building looking for a parking place where she could watch what went on. The detective wondered who lived here and what Rosemary was doing here. She didn't have to wonder long, Mr. Martin drove up fifteen minutes after Rosemary arrived. and drove into the underground garage, Ann had to stay all night and most of the next day. It was late Sunday afternoon when they both left in their separate cars. Well that's settled thought Ann, Martin is having an affair with the lady accountant although just how much of a lady is debatable.

Ann drove to the Police Station and found that Connally wasn't there. She walked to Detective Moore's office, the door was open so she walked in, knocking on the door as she walked past. David looked up from his desk and asked "Anything to report about last night?" Ann grinned mischievously and answered, "You were right, Martin and the lady accountant are having an affair. They have a little love nest across the river in Ohio in a relatively new housing development".

"Wow! Who would have thought they would go to such lengths! She has an apartment in Huntington and he has a condo, I wonder how long it's been going on?"

"She didn't carry a suitcase so I assume they keep clothes there which sounds like they've had it a while. I always wonder in cases like this, why murder seems to be the answer when divorce is a much better solution."

"That depends on how much money is involved" replied David.

"What's money if you're caught and spend the rest of your life in prison or end up in the gas chamber?" reasoned Ann.

"I'll bring the chief up to speed tomorrow but he'll want to see you. Now go home and get some sleep and good work detective!"

CHAPTER 10

Stuart hadn't seen Jenny for several days, not since that episode on the elevator. Where had she gone? Thoughts of Jenny as a ghost had interfered with her job and completely unnerved her. She decided she needed a jog in the park to clear her mind. It was getting cold now so she would need to dress warmly. It was Saturday and the park might be crowded but Stuart decided to go anyway.

She jogged a mile and then remembered that she needed to go to the drugstore and the grocery store. The jog had helped her spirits a little but she was still confused and annoyed. Nothing like this had ever happened to her. She couldn't tell David, she couldn't even tell her family, nobody believed in ghosts and she never did either......... until now?

Stuart picked up bread, milk, and some bananas at the grocery store and scotch tape at the drugstore. She parked her car in the garage and took the elevator to the tenth floor. No Jenny this time either, where had she gone? If there were any new suspects or leads in the case David wasn't forthcoming. Stuart hadn't heard from him since they had dinner at the Iron Horse. Her work had kept her busy and she assumed his work on the murder had kept him busy around the clock. When you were investigating murder there was no such thing as 'free' time. She wondered if Jenny could help solve the case. Where was she the night Mrs. Martin was killed? She was probably the only one awake while it happened but then it didn't happen on the elevator and the killer probably didn't use the elevator to escape. She had so many questions for Jenny, where had she gone?

As soon as David got to the Station he went to Chief Connally's office to tell him what Detective Derrick had found. "The report on the plumbers' fingerprints has come back and they do belong to the two plumbers from Sims and Sims." said the chief "It's good to know we have an answer to that problem but that means we're back to Waxler and maybe Martin, what did Detective Derrick find out over the weekend?"

"The grieving widower has a love nest across the river in Ohio and it seems he's had it for some time. Ann spent all night Saturday and most of Sunday parked outside, she'll tell you all about it when she gets here. Now we have two suspects either could have done it, Waxler for the coins or Martin instead of a divorce settlement. Why don't we get a search warrant for Waxler's place and see what we find and at the same time make Martin feel safe and unsuspected?" proposed David.

"I was just going to suggest that." answered the chief, "We have enough to pick him up so we'll do the search and arrest him at the same time."

David and two policemen arrived at Mr. Waxler's apartment about 2 pm,. David rang the door bell and John Waxler answered the door and seemed genuinely surprised to see them. "Can I help you?" asked John Waxler.

"We have a search warrant for your apartment" answered David.

"What do you hope to find? I had nothing to do with Mrs. Martin's death. I liked her."

"I'm sorry" said David, "We'll be as neat and fast as we can."

"Should I call a lawyer?" asked Mr. Waxler.

"It wouldn't be a bad idea." replied David. Mr. Waxler picked up his cell phone and walked into the kitchen. He dialed Stuart's number at work. "This is Stuart Browning."

"This is John Waxler, Miss Stuart, the police are here with a search warrant which looks to be legal, what should I do?"

"You have to let them search, but beyond that I'll have to ask my boss, Mr. Dobbs, I'll call you right back" offered Stuart. When Mr. Waxler got off the phone and turned around he was facing the detective. David read him his rights and then arrested him on suspicion of murder.

"I didn't kill Mrs. Martin! I liked her, I couldn't kill anybody!" pleaded Waxler "I want to call a lawyer!"

"You can call a lawyer from the station." David told him. Stuart called Mr. Waxler back but got no answer, she even had the operator check the line and it was not busy. That worried her but she didn't know what to do. In another few minutes her phone rang again.

"Miss Browning, they've arrested me for Mrs. Martin's murder! I'm at the police station. Can you get me a lawyer?"

"Don't worry Mr. Waxler I'll get a lawyer there right away." Stuart hung up the phone and sat a moment trying to make sense of Mr. Waxler's arrest. Surely David didn't think he had murdered Mrs. Martin. She had better talk to Mr. Dobbs right now and get Mr. Waxler a lawyer. She walked across the hall to Mr. Dobbs' office and asked his secretary if she could see him immediately. The secretary used her intercom to announce Stuart's request. "What's wrong Stuart?" asked Robert Dobbs.

"Mr. Waxler, our condo manager, has been arrested on suspicion of Mrs. Martin's murder and is being held at the police station now and he needs a lawyer."

"As you know, this firm doesn't practice criminal law but I'll be glad to go to the police station and see what I can do." replied Mr. Dobbs.

When Robert Dobbs arrived at the police station, John Waxler was in the interrogation room. Robert told the police that he was representing John and wished to see him alone. He entered the room and the questioning detective left.

"Tell me what evidence they have against you," asked the attorney.

"I don't know." answered Waxler, "They came in with a search warrant for my apartment and a few minutes later arrested me for murder. I can't imagine why they would suspect me!" Robert accompanied him to the magistrate court where he pled "not guilty". His case was then bound over to the Grand Jury and he was taken back to jail.

Stuart still had not heard anything from Mr. Dobbs before she left the office for the day. She thought about going to the police station but then thought better about it and went home. Surely Mr. Dobbs would call and tell her what went on at the police station. She pulled into her parking space in the garage, took the elevator to the tenth floor and went into her condo. She would just have to wait by the phone until Mr. Dobbs called.

CHAPTER 11

Stuart stood waiting for the elevator and looking as though she hadn't slept all night. Those shiny brass doors opened and there stood Jenny "Where have you been and do you know what has happened?" demanded Stuart.

"I know that nice Mr. Waxler has been arrested" answered Jenny "and he didn't do it."

"What do you know about the murder?" asked Stuart.

"I just know that Mr. Waxler didn't kill anybody." said Jenny.

"I'm sure he didn't do it either but we need some evidence to prove he didn't." continued Stuart.

"Have you talked to your detective friend?"

"Not since we had dinner last week." replied Stuart and then continued "Are you sure you don't know something?"

"I didn't see who did it, if that's what you mean," answered Jenny. The doors opened and Stuart was in the garage.

"We need to talk again." said Stuart as she got off the elevator.

The office was buzzing about the arrest of Mr. Waxler when Stuart arrived.

"What do you know?" everyone asked.

"I know that Mr. Waxler didn't murder Mrs. Martin" replied Stuart, "is Mr. Dobbs here yet?"

"Yes, I'm here," answered Robert Dobbs as he came to his office doorway. Stuart walked back and into his office.

"Thank you for going to see about Mr. Waxler last evening," Stuart began "what went on and how is he?"

"Well, what the police have is all circumstantial, no 'smoking gun' but enough to hold him." answered Robert.

"What do they have?" asked Stuart.

"First, he has keys to the Martin condo and to all the doors going into the building and he knew about the coins, second he's left-handed and it's been established that the murderer is left-handed, and lastly, he has no alibi for the night of the murder. He says he was home alone. I don't believe he did it but it will take more than that to get him released."

"He has keys to all of our condos and to the outside doors as well, he has to he's the manager, so that can be discounted." offered Stuart.

"That still leaves his knowing about the coins and being left handed and needing an alibi for the night of the murder," added Robert Dobbs, "plus the fact that there's no sign of an outside entry anyplace in the building, so it would seem to be an inside job."

"I'm almost positive he didn't do it but I don't know how to go about proving it" said Stuart.

"We will have to find a good criminal lawyer for him, I promised that I would and I will. I have a friend who practices criminal law in the eastern panhandle and he's very good, we went to law school together. His cases often take him into Washington, D.C. He's expensive but I'll ask him anyway because I don't think John Waxler did it."

"I'd better get to work" said Stuart as she turned to leave his office. She had already decided to call David so when she sat down at her desk she dialed his number at work.

"This is detective Moore."

"David, this is Stuart, I would like to talk to you about the case and I'm wondering if you could stop by this evening? "

"Yes, but it might be nine or nine-thirty, is that too late?"

"No, that's fine, I'll see you tonight." Stuart put down the phone and began to ponder all the things that Robert Dobbs had told her. If there were no signs of a forced entry into the building then it would appear to be an inside job, but Mr. Waxler? Couldn't be.

Stuart was anxious to get on the elevator to talk to Jenny again. She was convinced that Jenny knew something. After parking her car in the garage, Stuart headed for the elevator. When the brass doors opened she quickly looked for Jenny but alas Jenny wasn't there, She was so unpredictable!! This had been a trying day all the way around but maybe David could turn it into a better evening.

There was chicken in the refrigerator so Stuart made a chicken sandwich and a salad. She made extra coffee so David could have a cup when he came. The time crept by but at nine o'clock the buzzer sounded and Stuart got up and pushed the button to open the front door to the building. Once again she opened her front door and waited for David to step off the elevator. "Hello Stuart, how are you?" asked David as he got off the elevator.

"Right now I'm worried about Mr. Waxler, come in." answered Stuart.

David followed her inside where she took his coat and hung it in the closet. She offered him a chair and asked if he would like a cup of coffee. "Yes, I'd like a cup and black, please." answered David as he sat down. Stuart disappeared into the kitchen to get the coffee. She returned shortly carrying a tray holding the coffee, cups, napkins, and a plate of brownies. After she had poured both coffees and offered David the brownies she sat down.

"You can't possibly believe that Mr. Waxler killed Mrs. Martin." began Stuart.

"Well, he's been arrested for suspicion of murder so what I think doesn't matter, there's enough evidence against him for an arrest." said David.

"What can I do to help him?" asked Stuart.

"Find the real murderer if you think he's innocent," proposed David, "and if that's not possible then get him the best criminal lawyer you can find, I do have some information I can share with you but you can't tell your lawyers just yet."

"Quick, tell me what you know." urged Stuart.

"We've had Mr. Martin shadowed, after what you heard, and he's having an affair with a woman in his office and that makes him a suspect but not enough of a suspect to release Waxler yet, but you can rest a little easier."

"Mr. Dobbs has already located a good criminal lawyer but I don't want it to go trial. He's innocent and we've got to prove it." answered Stuart.

David could see that she was upset so he tried to change the subject, "My chief says that there are condo rules here that could keep robberies from happening, could you tell me about these rules?"

"Well," started Stuart, "no owner is ever supposed to let anyone have a key to the front entrance to the building. Our keys to our own front doors can be given to anyone we want but the keys to our entrance to the building can never be given to non owners since that entrance is everyone's front door. That's our first line of defense you might say, if one key is given out, then that puts all the rest of us in jeopardy. And that entrance key opens all the outside doors as well."

"Do you think that any of your neighbors might have given an entrance key to anyone, perhaps a member of the family or a friend?" questioned David.

"No, I don't think so, that would be very selfish. If they did they don't belong in a condominium, they belong in a house alone." answered Stuart, "I think my neighbors are too smart and too thoughtful to do anything that foolhardy."

"If that's true and everyone follows the rules, then that sounds worse for John Waxler" David mused.

"I know it does," agreed Stuart "but I still believe he couldn't have done it. Don't you think he would have had an alibi in place if he were guilty?"

"You would think so." answered David.

"May I get more coffee for you?" asked Stuart.

"No, thank you" replied David. "I must be going, it's getting late." Stuart got his coat and walked to her front door with him. David put on his coat and thanked her for the coffee and brownies.

"Your information has made me feel better about Mr. Waxler's case." said Stuart as she opened the door. "Let's keep sharing information".

"Oh, I will." replied David as he walked to the elevator.

CHAPTER 12

Stuart could hardly wait to talk to Mr. Dobbs who had been out of the office when she arrived earlier. She knew that his friend, the lawyer from the eastern panhandle, had decided to take Mr. Waxler's case. She wondered what this new attorney thought about Mr. Waxler and the case. She asked Mr. Dobbs secretary to let her know when Mr. Dobbs arrived.

Sam Dixon had arrived at the police station to speak to his new client. He and Robert Dobbs had arrived together but Sam did all the questioning. He had already gone over Robert's file on the case so it was really just a preliminary meeting between attorney and client.

As they left the jail Sam asked Robert, "May I use your office and your paralegal while I'm on this case?"

"Of course, and my paralegal resides in the same building as your client so she may be helpful in building a defense for Waxler." answered Robert. "She thinks he's innocent."

"What do you really think?" asked Sam.

"There's only circumstantial evidence against him and he has no criminal record so I'm inclined to believe him."

"I feel the same way." responded Sam. Stuart saw the two men walk into Dobbs office and hoped that Mr. Dobbs would call her soon. Her intercom sounded and she was asked to come to Mr. Dobbs office. She was introduced to Sam Dixon and told that she would be helping him with the case if she elected to, which she replied with a resounding "Yes! I want to help because I know he's innocent."

"Other than liking the man, do you have any evidence to substantiate his innocence?" questioned Sam Dixon.

"No, but I'm trying to uncover some." answered Stuart.

"You'll be a help because you believe in his innocence." Sam told her.

Stuart returned to her office and felt better about Mr. Waxler's chances. She liked this new lawyer and felt that he would do his best to clear John Waxler of the charges.

Chief Connally called David to his office and when he got there the chief told him to have a seat. "John Waxler has a criminal attorney from the eastern panhandle and he's supposed to be very good." explained the chief.

"That must make Stuart Browning happy since she believes that Waxler is innocent." commented David.

"The prosecutor has asked us to go over the evidence again and see if we can come up with more evidence and maybe find something new." said the chief.

"I've been over CSI evidence several times and I can't find anything more, those guys are pretty thorough." answered David.

"There's still nothing more on the husband, is there?"

"Only that he's still having an affair with Miss Howard." replied David.

"It would tighten the case against Waxler if we could just find the murder weapon, but I know that you searched his apartment from top to bottom and couldn't find anything." said the chief.

"I don't think he threw it into the Ohio River that would be too "iffy" he lives too far from the river, but I can't even guess where he did stash it." David said with a sigh.

"I guess we've helped the prosecutor all we can right now, continue to work the case and maybe something more will turn up on Mr. Martin and his motive.""

CHAPTER 13

Stuart had parked her car in the garage and was waiting for the elevator. The shining brass doors opened and there stood Jenny.

"Where have you been?" asked Stuart as the elevator started its upward journey, "We need to talk."

"Has something new happened?" asked Jenny.

"No, that's just it, if something doesn't happen soon Mr. Waxler could go to prison for murder. I know why I want to help him but why do you? You seem to have more than just a passing interest in the case, does it hold some of those answers that you're looking for?"

"Yes, but not in the way you think, I want to help Mr. Waxler because he's a nice man and I know he couldn't have done it. But there is one thing I know for certain, the key to this murder is on the sixth floor."

"The key to the murder is on the sixth floor? CSI was all over that condo with a fine tooth comb." said Stuart.

"I know," answered Jenny, "but I still say the key to the murder is on the sixth floor." The elevator stopped on the tenth floor and Stuart got off. She turned back to Jenny and said "Thank you for trying to help and if you think of anything else, something more than 'the sixth floor' get in touch with me."

David called Stuart to have dinner and told her that he would pick her up at seven. Stuart knew that Jenny was trying to help but one sentence wouldn't quite do it. Should she tell David? Yes and no. Maybe CSI missed something but could they or would they search the Martin condo again? She must find a way to ask David.

Stuart was waiting and David was on time as usual. She had decided to meet him downstairs and save time. They drove to the "Iron Horse" again and got a booth close to the fireplace. It was a cold and wintry night and just looking at the fire made the room feel warmer. After their drinks arrived David asked Stuart about a New Years Eve party that her condo association had every year.

"As you know this will be my first new years eve in Huntington but I've been told that the association has a dance every year with a local combo entertaining and they serve drinks and finger food."

"That sounds like fun." said David "I wonder if I could go along as your date and observe your neighbors? I might learn something to help John Waxler."

"Certainly," replied Stuart, "and if you like to dance, so much the better."

Their steaks arrived and while they ate dinner Stuart mulled over asking David if CSI could go over the Martin condo again. Finally she asked, "David, is CSI positive they recovered all the evidence in the Martin condo on the sixth floor?"

"Yes," answered David, "why do you ask?"

"Well, I have a friend who wants to remain anonymous and seems to be sure that the key to the murder is on the sixth floor."

"What does he or she have in mind, do you know?"

"She just wants to help Mr. Waxler and she seems certain that CSI didn't find all the evidence."

"It's highly unusual if they didn't find everything. I'll look over their report again and see what I come up with. Did she say why she thinks CSI missed something during their investigation?"

"No," answered Stuart "she just seems to think there is an important clue still on the sixth floor."

"Does this anonymous friend live in the building?" asked David.

"No, she just visits but she likes Mr. Waxler a lot" replied Stuart.

"What would make her think that CSI didn't recover all the evidence?"

"I don't know," answered Stuart "but she seemed very sure."

"You're not going to tell me her name, are you?" asked David.

"I can't, I promised." said Stuart "besides that's not important, only the clue is."

"How can I help Waxler or solve this case if there's someone with information who won't come forth?" demanded David.

"I know, I'm sorry, but I'm not so sure how good her information is and we have to solve this murder by whatever means possible." replied Stuart.

After dinner their coffee arrived and David changed the subject, "How do I dress for this New Years Eve function?"

"Well, from what I hear it's a black tie affair. It's only a week away, you know, so I'd better turn in our reservation tomorrow. I might finally get to know some of my neighbors." answered Stuart.

As David was driving home after taking Stuart home he began to wonder about her anonymous friend. He stopped by the station before heading home to look at the CSI report again. He parked outside the station and walked in speaking to the desk sergeant on duty. When he got to his office he looked through his files for the CSI report. He read the report again and found nothing new. Who was this anonymous friend and what was her connection with the murder? Questions without answers. Both Stuart and the chief want to find clues that CSI missed, why do they both think something was missed?

CHAPTER 14

It was a perfect New Years Eve. The snow was falling quietly and in the black sky above the stars sparkled like diamonds. David parked his car in the parking lot of the condo building and as he got out he felt magic in the air. He rang Stuart's number and waited for the familiar buzz that unlocked the front entrance. As Stuart pushed the button in her condo to let David inside she tried to imagine how he would look in a tux. She opened her front door and waited for the elevator to stop on the tenth floor, David stepped out looking as good as she had imagined. He stopped short and exclaimed "Whoa! You look good enough to eat!"

"Why thank you" answered Stuart as she flushed slightly. After spending the last week trying to decide what to wear, Stuart had chosen a strapless red taffeta floor length gown and had piled her hair high on her head. She had added crystal chandelier earrings and was carrying a silver evening bag. "I'll lock the door and we'll go down." said Stuart.

David pushed the button for the elevator and waited for Stuart to join him. Those shining doors opened and Stuart was again reminded of the elegance of this elevator with its brass railing, walnut walls and of course its red carpet, just perfect for Jenny the ghost.

They exited the elevator on the lobby floor and walked to the doorway of the party room. There they were greeted by a sea of faces and the buzz of conversation. The combo was in front of a long floor to ceiling window and a door opening onto a deck beside the pool, the bar was on one side of the room, and the table with the finger food was opposite the bar on another long wall. There were tables covered with white cloths scattered around the room. The middle of the room was for dancing. The decorations were very New Years Eve, colored balloons covered the ceiling and a very large silver "Happy New Year" hung over the combo and on each table were hats and noisemakers for the 'bewitching hour'.

"Shall I get the drinks?" asked David.

"Yes," answered Stuart, "but I'll go along, you've met all these people during your interrogations but I haven't so you can do the introductions.

"Sounds fair, come on with me."

A pathway opened up as they made their way to the bar, everyone recognized the good-looking detective but were surprised to see him at the party. Most of the residents did not know Stuart, especially in a formal dress with her hair worn up instead of down but they thought she must be the new owner on the tenth floor. As they passed through the crowd there were several "good evening detective" from the men who recognized him. David got a glass of red wine for himself and a glass of white wine for Stuart. They stood talking for a minute when a man approached them and asked if they would join his table. David answered that they would be happy to join them. The three of them made their way to the table where David introduced the man, Bob Hancock, to Stuart. Then Bob Hancock introduced his wife, Elizabeth, to Stuart. The other two at the table were Jean and Hank Symes. They all sat down and Hank asked with a grin, "Can I assume you're not on duty detective?" David held up his glass and answered, "You assume correctly, I'm here to have a good time and enjoy the company of a beautiful woman."

"Here, here!" said Bob Hancock as he lifted his glass in salute.

The music was playing slowly as Stuart and David approached the dance floor. When he took her in his arms Stuart could feel the strength of this man, not just his physical strength but the respect he generated from the other people present. The charm of a man lay in his strength so that made David a most charming man. He was also an accomplished dancer and easy to follow. They enjoyed dancing together and did it well.

Stuart danced with the other men at the table while David danced with their wives. Everyone wanted to talk to David about the case and he did find out a few things that had not come to light before. It seemed that a few people did not like John Waxler and thought he could be guilty, however they had no facts to back up their feelings. To be entirely factual none of them knew what Waxler did with his free time.

It was five minutes to midnight so everybody began to put on their hats and get their noisemakers ready for midnight. David looked at Stuart and whispered "You know I'll have to kiss you if we're to look like real dates." The drum roll sounded and a new year was here. David leaned down and said "Happy New Year" and kissed her softly but lingered a moment longer than just a friend would do. Stuart was speechless for a few seconds but recovered her composure enough to say "Happy New Year" to him. A wonderful evening just got better.

CHAPTER 15

Sam Dixon was in Robert Dobb's office when Stuart arrived for work. He had gone home for New Years but was back on the job today. He asked Robert's secretary to have Stuart come to his office.

"You wanted to see me?" asked Stuart as she entered his office.

"Yes" answered Sam "I wanted to ask you if you had learned anything at the New Years Eve party?"

" Not really, but I did find that a small number of my neighbors feel that Mr. Waxler could be guilty."

"Do you know why they feel that way?"

"No, I think it's just a case of not everyone likes everybody, they don't need a reason." explained Stuart.

"Do you think any of your neighbors would be willing to testify in Waxler's defense, as to his character, truthfulness, honesty, you know the drill."

"Yes, I'm sure they would." replied Stuart "but we need real proof of his innocence and where do we find it?"

"Maybe I should give you a copy of the CSI report. You could study it and maybe find something we could hang our hats on. I'll get my copy and you can make a copy for yourself" offered Sam.

"The prosecution hasn't found the weapon or the coins but they're turning over every rock to look," Stuart informed him.

Stuart started home with the CSI report after work, she intended to study it tonight. After parking her car she pressed the button for the elevator. The brass doors opened and Stuart got on. Before she could make her tenth floor selection Jenny spoke up "Hi, Stuart, did you all have a good time at the dance?"

"Jenny, I need to talk to you but wait until I press ten" replied Stuart. "Yes, I had a wonderful evening at the dance, the music was good and I got to meet most of my neighbors." answered Stuart as she held up the folder and told Jenny. "Here's the CSI report of the murder scene, I'll find out what they found on the sixth floor and hope I can figure out your clue that's on the sixth floor."

"Good luck." said Jenny. "The key to this murder is still on the sixth floor and you've got to find it. you can help both Mr. Waxler and me."

"How can I help you? I feel you have more than just a passing interest in the case. Do you know something I don't? when I finish this report how do I find you?" asked Stuart.

"I'll find you." answered Jenny as the doors opened on the tenth floor.

Stuart opened her condo door and went inside she left her CSI folder in the living room and went into her bedroom to change clothes. After changing her clothes she went back into the living room, picked up the report and sat down in a comfortable chair to study it. Mrs. Martin's body had not been moved and there was blood on the carpet in a large circle around her head but the murder weapon was not found or identified. Nothing in the condo had been disturbed with the exception of the master bedroom closet, the coins had been kept in the closet in a box but of course they were gone so that must have been the motive. Unidentified prints had been found in the condo but not in the closet. Those prints had now been identified as belonging to the plumbers who had replaced the hot water tank. The killer must have been wearing gloves or else there would have been prints in the closet, mused Stuart. And it's obvious that Mrs. Martin surprised the burglar in her condo, which would have put the time at about ten-forty five. The coins had already been stolen and the thief was on his way out when Mrs. Martin returned. The front door was unlocked when Mr. Martin returned home but why would the murderer stop to lock the door…he wouldn't. That was the entire scenario and it pointed to someone inside the building, if not, how did someone get into the building? Jenny can attest to the fact that the killer did not use the elevator to come and go, but only she and I know that. We know that he must have used the stairs but Jenny can't testify and even if she could that only makes John Waxler look guiltier. Why does Jenny keep saying that the key to the murder is on the sixth floor?

Stuart pondered whom she could get to testify for John Waxler as a character witness. She thought probably the Hancocks and the Symes, they both seemed to think highly of him. Character witnesses just weren't enough, he had no alibi for the night of the murder and he knew about the coins in the condo. Did the CSI search the stairwell for clues? thought Stuart, maybe she should search the stairwell from the sixth floor to the lobby and see if anything incriminating could be found. Of course she didn't know what to look for, just something that seemed to be out of place. She would do that tomorrow. it was past her bedtime, she had been going over this CSI report for hours so she finally decided to go to bed.

It was another cold morning when Stuart awoke. Snow flurries were blowing everywhere but last night the TV weatherman had said there would be no accumulation. As she dressed for work she thought about the CSI report again, maybe this evening when she returned from work she would check the stairwell. She would also call the Hancocks and the Symes and ask them to be character witnesses for John Waxler.

Stuart pushed the button for the elevator and stood waiting. The shining brass doors opened and there stood Jenny. "Did you learn anything from the report?"

"No, do you have any idea how the killer got to the sixth floor since you didn't see him on the elevator?"

"No." answered Jenny. "He didn't ride the elevator so he must have walked up the stairs".

"After I get home tonight I'm going to examine the stairwell and see if I can find anything. although I'm sure the CSI would have examined it already."

David walked into the chief's office to report about New Years Eve. The chief looked over the top of his glasses and motioned him to sit down. "Well, did you learn anything we didn't already know?"

"No, not really, but I got questioned... a lot."

"Did people believe that you were just there on a date?"

"I think so, Stuart was a knockout in a fabulous red dress, people couldn't help but believe that I was on a real date."

"It sounds that way just hearing you say it. Are you falling for that girl or have you already fallen?" asked the chief. "Just be sure you keep your mind on your work, boy."

"Oh, I can handle it." answered David with a smile.

CHAPTER 16

Stuart got home from work and changed into a warm-up suit. If she were going to walk down the stairs from the sixth floor to the lobby she wanted warm, comfortable clothes. Since she didn't want to attract attention, she decided to make her trip during the dinner hour while the other owners were inside having dinner.

She took the elevator from the tenth floor to the sixth floor hoping to see Jenny, but Jenny wasn't in the elevator. Stuart got off on the sixth floor and when she saw that yellow police tape over the door it startled her, that really brought her attention to the murder. The murderer had walked this same hall only a short time ago and poor Mrs. Martin had been murdered right behind that door! She didn't feel quite as brave as she had before the yellow tape reminded her that this was all part of a murder scene. She hurried to the stairwell and left this scene behind her, she opened the door and stepped in quickly and began by looking around the landing carefully but she didn't find anything. Then she started down the stairs to the fifth floor and examined each step as she went. No luck so far. As she started on down to the fourth floor she saw something in the corner she walked over and picked up a penny, a brand new one, usually that meant good luck but…..She made her way down the stairs to the lobby carefully examining each step. She knew now that if she were to find any clue to John's case or listen to Jenny's admonition that "the key was on the sixth floor" she must examine every place she knew the murderer had been after he had killed Mrs. Martin.

The only places she knew he had been were the stairs between the first and sixth floors, on the sixth floor, and in the Martin's condo. CSI had gone over the condo 'ad infinitum' and found nothing in the way of clues to the murderer's identity, she had just examined the stairway slowly and carefully so that just left the sixth floor itself. It would have to wait for another day, she was tired and she needed to think some more. She rode the elevator back up to the tenth floor but Jenny wasn't aboard this time, either.

After breakfast Stuart left her condo ready for work. She pushed the button and stood waiting. When the doors opened there stood Jenny. "Where have you been, I looked for you last night." said Stuart.

"Why, has something happened?" asked Jenny.

"No," answered Stuart "but after work I searched the stairwell between the sixth floor and the lobby."

"Did you find anything? That must have been the way he came and left, but I keep telling you that the key is only to be found on the sixth floor."

"I know, I know." responded Stuart "have you found any answer to your problem?"

"No, but when I do I will need your help, please think it over and help me, in the end it may help this case as well."

"Well, you need to give me a little more than 'the sixth floor' to find the clue." said Stuart as the elevator doors opened into the garage.

Stuart spoke to Mary Wilson as she walked back to her office. Then she buzzed Robert Dobbs' secretary to see if Sam Dixon were there yet, he wasn't so Stuart made calls to Bob Hancock and Hank Symes to ask them to testify in John Waxler's behalf. They both agreed to testify and hoped it would help. They wanted to know how the case was going and she didn't want to tell them that it wasn't going well so she just said, "We're working hard."

Stuart thought about going to see John Waxler after work just to see how his spirits were. He knew that she was working on his case but she hadn't seen him since before he went to jail. He was certain to be depressed about his situation but she couldn't tell him anything new. She'd like to tell him about Jenny and her help but she couldn't of course. She dared not tell anyone, she and Jenny would just have to solve this mystery themselves.

Sam Dixon stopped at Stuart's office on his way to Robert's office, "Nothing new, is there?" he asked.

"No," replied Stuart, "but I'd like to go and see Mr. Waxler this evening if you think it would be all right."

"I think he could use a new and pretty face to look at for a change so go right ahead."

"By the way, I talked to Mr. Hancock and Mr. Symes and they are both glad to testify on Mr. Waxler's behalf." she informed him.

Since Stuart had never visited a jail before she didn't exactly know what to do. Maybe she should ask for David? No, she would just tell the desk sergeant who she was and that she needed to see Mr. Dixon's client. An officer showed her to the Visitor's room and then left to get John Waxler. She sat down and waited, in just a few minutes the officer returned with Mr. Waxler and John seemed very glad to see her. The officer left and John sat down. "How are you?" Stuart asked.

"I want out of here," he answered "but I want to thank you for all your help getting Mr. Dobbs and then Mr. Dixon as my attorneys. I did not kill Mrs. Martin and Mr. Dixon seems to think he can prove it." said John.

"All of the owners are behind you and Mr. Hancock and Mr. Symes are going to testify as character witnesses for you." added Stuart.

"I had no reason to kill her, they've searched my apartment for the missing coins and found nothing, what does Mr. Martin think of me?"

"He's kept pretty much to himself and from I've heard he has not said anything, one way or the other." replied Stuart, "Do you think he could have had something to do with his wife's murder?"

"No, I don't, they always seemed happily married to me, besides he was still out of town when it happened."

"I know, he has a rock solid alibi for that night, is there anything you need or anything you want me to do for you?" asked Stuart.

"No, thank you, I don't need much in here." he answered.

"Well, I'll go now but I want you to know that we're all working hard and you'll be out of here in no time." she assured him. She wished she believed that, she thought as she left the room.

As she drove home she thought about examining the sixth floor tonight, around midnight would probably be the best time everyone would be asleep by then. She parked her car in the garage and walked to the elevator. The doors opened but Jenny wasn't there so she couldn't talk over her plan for tonight.

Stuart had a hard time waiting for midnight to come. About eleven o'clock she had gotten real sleepy, that was her normal time to go to bed. The excitement of what she might find opened her eyes quickly though. She thought about taking the elevator down to six but decided against it lest someone hear the noise. That must have been what the murderer thought too. She walked down to the sixth floor and opened the door carefully. Everything was quiet so she stepped out of the stairwell and closed the door quickly. She saw that yellow tape and it made her feel creepy and uneasy again but she walked to 603 and started there, the murderer must have walked from the door of 603 to the door she had just come thru. The elevator was between the stairwell and 603.

Just outside the door of 603 was a large decorative tree that took up a lot of room. A space about 4ft by 4ft had been cut out of the marble floor and artificial dirt and grass about 5 inches deep surrounded the tree. It was the same on all the floors, there was a tree at either end of the corridor. Stuart looked closely at the area around the door and began backing away and looking down at the floor as she neared the tree. What was that shining in the dirt? "P-s-s-s-t," came a whisper, Stuart caught her breath and froze, afraid to move. In the quiet of the midnight hour it was eerie being alone in this corridor, but she turned around anxiously, expecting the worst, and saw Jenny standing in the elevator motioning her to come inside. She walked into the elevator and before she could speak, Jenny shut the doors and whispered "Somebody is waiting for the elevator in the lobby, I'm taking you up to the tenth floor and we'll talk later." The elevator whizzed up, the doors opened, Stuart got out and Jenny was gone again.

He smiled to himself as he realized the authorities were closing in on that condo manager, Waxler. They had no idea who the real murderer was, they assumed they already had him. He thought that even he himself would suspect Waxler, with all the circumstantial evidence and no alibi. But of course he knew better, he knew everything about that night, from entering the door on the deck to leaving the building by the same door.

He had sighed with relief when he turned over the coins to his bookie. He had owed him more money than he could ever have repaid. He *MUST* control his habit but whenever and wherever the 'ponies' ran he had to have some money ridin' with 'em!......... a lucky thing, though, the coins were out of his possession now so there was no way to connect him to the crime. He enjoyed thinking about all the ways that Fate had helped him. No one had heard him come and go, no one knew how he had gotten in, no one knew how he had gotten rid of the coins and the authorities had a good case against that manager and had stopped looking any further. He was sure one lucky man!

CHAPTER 17

Stuart was awakened by her phone, she looked at the clock and it read 7a.m.she answered the ring and it was Mr. Dobbs. He wanted her to stop by the courthouse on her way to work. It seemed that Mrs. Martin had been left a large sum of money at her parents' deaths and he wanted to know how much. This had never come up before. Mr. Dobbs wanted her to look up the wills of Mrs. Martin's parents and also look up Mrs. Martin's and see who inherited at her death. Mr. Waxler had just happened to mention to Sam Dixon that Mrs. Martin 'came from money.' Dixon seized on that right away and called Mr. Dobbs to confirm the particulars.

As Stuart dressed for work she thought about how the tables were beginning to turn for Mr. Waxler. She had to get back to the sixth floor as soon as she could and examine that shiny object she had seen last evening before Jenny had whisked her away. When could she get back? After work and during the dinner hour, perhaps today? Oh, most assuredly today, she had to know what that shiny object was!

Stuart walked into the courthouse and to the section concerning Wills. Mr. Dobbs had given her the dates of the Wills and the names to look under. She found the Will books and searched for the right years. Finally she carried two large ledgers back to a table and began her search. Mr. Waxler was correct, Mrs. Martin came from money all right, she had inherited $1,000,000 from her parents. People had been murdered for a lot less! Now to look up Mrs. Martin's Will, that was easier since it had been filed recently. Back she came to the table with another large ledger. Just as Mr. Dobbs had suspected, everything was left to Mr. Martin by Mrs. Martin's Will. Stuart put all the Ledgers back in place and left the Courthouse.

Mr. Dixon was waiting in Mr. Dobbs office to hear Stuart's report. "Got it,." said Stuart excitedly as she rushed into the office. "We have reasonable doubt."

"Hold on there." responded Mr. Dixon with a smile. "Tell me all about it." Stuart sat down and pulled out her notebook.

"Mrs. Martin's parents left her $1,000,000, and she in turn left it all to Mr. Martin and that's a lot more motive than $10,000!"

"You're right," answered Mr. Dixon, "it is a lot more motive and I think it's enough for reasonable doubt, good work Miss Browning.

Stuart didn't know whether to tell David or not, he was part of the enemy wasn't he? She knew that Mr. Dixon wouldn't approve. The police weren't really the enemy, of course, but they worked for the prosecution. She had found them to be very fair and they would look into any clues that she found. Maybe she could hint to David that the police might look at Mrs. Martin's Will and see if Mr. Martin had anything to gain from Mrs. Martin's death. Then she thought about the shiny object on the sixth floor , she had to get back to it this evening.

Stuart called David and suggested that he check and see what Mr. Martin gained, if anything, from Mrs. Martin's death. "We all know about the insurance policy, that it's not worth much but maybe Mrs. Martin's will could shed some light on a motive for Mr. Martin." She hated to think that but David had alluded in the beginning that Martin was a suspect. David hopped on that news right away, he seemed genuinely impressed and promised to follow up on it quickly but not give away his "source".

David hurried to the courthouse and looked up Mrs. Martin's Will. It left everything to Mr. Martin but what did Mrs. Martin have to leave? Then he discovered what Stuart had found..........$1,000,000! He rushed back to the station to tell the Chief they had their motive and was it a big one.

After doing some routine work for Mr. Dobbs that took most of the afternoon, Stuart prepared to wrap up her day and go home. She parked her car in the garage and got on the elevator. The doors closed and there stood Jenny. "Am I glad to see you." exclaimed Stuart, "I have good news, we've raised reasonable doubt about Mr. Waxler's guilt. Mr. Martin has inherited $1,000,000 from Mrs. Martin's Will."

"Wonderful," answered Jenny "Now you've got to go back to the sixth floor and see about that shiny object.

"I'm going to go back about six or six-thirty while everyone's having dinner, what do you think?" asked Stuart.

"I think that's a good time, I'll keep watch and come to get you if anyone appears to be going to the sixth floor."

"You scared me to death last night!" exclaimed Stuart.

"I know and I'm sorry but I didn't have much time." answered Jenny. They arrived at the tenth floor and the doors opened "See you later." said Jenny as Stuart got off. Stuart opened her door and went inside. She walked to the kitchen and got a drink of water and there on the counter lay a forgotten Hershey bar, just what she needed. Now to change her clothes while she enjoyed her candy bar.

By six o'clock Stuart was dressed and ready for her foray on the sixth floor. She walked down to the sixth floor so as not to attract attention by the elevator noise. She went directly to the ornamental tree closest to 603. There, by looking carefully, she saw the shiny object she had seen last night. She got down on her knees so she could see better and blew a little of the dirt away. There lay a key...... a gold key. *THE* key on the sixth floor.... *THE KEY* to the murder? Stuart carefully covered it again and carefully didn't touch it. She had to call David. After taking the elevator up to the tenth floor, without seeing Jenny, she went into her condo to phone David.

"David," Stuart began "You've got to come over here as soon as you can, I've found something important to the case so bring gloves and an envelope."

"I'll be right there." answered David. He knew that Stuart would never call him to come over if it weren't important.

David pushed Stuart's number and waited to be admitted. She buzzed him in immediately and he took the elevator to the tenth floor. There she stood in the doorway waiting. "Come in, come in." invited Stuart anxiously. She shut the door and motioned him to a chair while she sat down opposite him,. "Do you remember when I told you that I had a friend who insisted that the key to the murder was on the sixth floor?" Stuart asked.

"Sure, I remember, but there's no proof that CSI overlooked anything."

"Well," Stuart continued, "I've found the key on the sixth floor, is it the key to the murder? I don't know but it's a real key that unlocks a real door and we won't know anymore unless or until you check it for fingerprints."

"Let's go." answered David as he stood up. They got on the elevator and there stood Jenny! Stuart gasped in shock and disbelief but before she could say anything Jenny spoke up, "Quiet Stuart, he can't see me or hear me only you can, I just want to be sure that you find the key," Before Stuart could catch her breath the elevator stopped on six. They got off and Stuart led the way to the tree. There under the tree and partially covered by the artificial grass was the shiny object that Stuart thought was a key. She had carefully covered it and had not touched it. They got down on their knees together and David put on the rubber gloves, he brushed the grass and the dirt away and there it was….a shiny gold key. He turned to Stuart to say something but her face was so close to his that he kissed her instead, tenderly like a man in love. They looked at each other for a long minute while David held her close, "I think we just found that key I called you about," said Stuart as she slowly drew away from his embrace. David pulled out a small envelope from his coat pocket and deposited the key inside and then suddenly he turned the envelope upside down and dumped the key back into his hand, "Does it look familiar to you?" he asked Stuart.

"No, it just looks like a key." she answered.

"No, no." continued David "that's not what I mean, do you have your keys with you?"

"Yes."

"May I have them a minute?"

"Of course, here." she said as she handed over her key ring.

"What does this one key fit?"

"Why it's the key to the condo building." Stuart told him.

"That's what I thought, the key we just found is identical to your condo key!"

"Who could have lost his condo key and why hadn't it been reported?" Stuart asked, mostly to herself.

"Nobody would have hidden the condo key here, maybe their own door key but not the condo door key." said David with a puzzled look. "I've got to get back to the CSI lab and have it tested for prints."

"I don't suppose I could come with you?" asked Stuart, "After all I found it."

"No, that's against policy but I'll call you the minute I find out anything."

He gave Stuart her keys and pressed the button for the elevator. As the doors opened Stuart got in saying "We'll go to the lobby I want you to get started on those fingerprints." The elevator coasted down to the lobby and David got out, turning around to look at Stuart once more before the doors closed.

Stuart pressed ten, stepped back, and her head filled with all kinds of excitement. This key might prove Mr. Waxler's innocence and was David in love with her? And was she falling in love with David?

CHAPTER 18

Last night David had jumped into his car and headed for the police station. When he got there he went directly to the CSI laboratory where they were working on another case. He cajoled one of the men into lifting the fingerprints from the key. There was a good thumb print on one side and a good forefinger print on the other side. This was lucky, usually the thumb print was good but often the forefinger print was smudged. The CSI was too busy to run the prints then but promised the chief detective that they would be run against the condo owners the first thing in the morning. David hated to wait until morning but he took back the key and placed it in the Martin file and left.

As Chief Connally was walking to his office to go over the cases for today one of the CSI stopped him, "chief, last evening Detective Moore brought us a key to have the fingerprints lifted and we did but we didn't have time to match them to other prints but this morning we did. We tried them against all the owners in the building and came up empty."

"What's this?" asked David as he walked through the chief's door.

"I was just telling the chief that I didn't find a match to the fingerprints you brought in last evening."

"Have you tried them against all the owners in the building?" David asked.

"Yep, and no match."

"Have you tried the prints of the two plumbers?" David kept on.

"No, are those with the owners' prints?"

"They're in the Martin file," replied David.

"I'll check them and get right back to you." promised the CSI.

"Well, what's this all about?" questioned the chief.

"Stuart Browning called yesterday about dinner time and told me that she had found a key on the sixth floor in the dirt surrounding a fake tree. She hadn't touched it and wanted me to come and see about it and possibly have it checked for prints."

"And of course you went running!" said the chief as he continued "so somebody lost a key so what?"

"So the prints don't match any of the owners or Waxler so whose are they and why was the key covered up in the dirt?" answered David.

"Now we have the mystery of the uncovered key?" said Connally as he turned his attention back to his desk. David lingered a moment and then left. The CSI came rushing back to David's office repeating over and over "It's a match, it's a match!"

"Who's the match?" asked David excitedly.

"It's the plumber, Harry Sessions, from Sims and Sims!"

"He's not supposed to have a key to the building, what's going on? Let's take this to the chief." Connally had just hung up his phone when the two men barged in.

"We've got a match," exclaimed David.

"Who?" questioned Connally.

"The plumber, Harry Sessions from Sims & Sims." answered David.

"Get Martin on the phone and ask if he or Mrs. Martin ever gave their building keys to anyone and to check and see if he still has two building keys." ordered Connally.

"I'm on it." replied David as he walked out the door. He sat down at his desk and dialed Martin's office. The secretary answered and he asked to speak to Mr. Martin. Martin came on the line immediately, "Yes detective?"

"We were just wondering if you ever gave anyone your key to the front door of your building?" asked David.

"Why, no, it's against our condominium rules." answered Martin.

"Do you still have your two original keys to the building?" questioned David.

"Yes" replied Martin, "Why do you ask?"

"Oh, we're just double checking everything." said the detective, "Sorry to bother you."

David hung up his phone and called Stuart at her office.

"This is Stuart Browning."

"Hey, it's me, I got those prints identified but you must promise not to tell anybody, it might scare him off."

"Whose are they?" Stuart asked excitedly.

"They belong to the plumber from Sims and Sims named Harry Sessions, and he has no business with that key." David told her.

"I knew it wasn't Mr. Waxler, somebody else just had to have a key, what are we going to do now?"

"Hold on there, Nancy Drew, I'll let you know as soon as I know." promised David.

He put down the phone and started to think about what they could do. Could they get a search warrant for Harry's home? Was the discovered key enough evidence for a warrant? He'd better talk to the chief. He walked down the hall to Connally's office and waited while the chief finished a conversation with another detective. "I got the information from Mr. Martin." started David.

"And?" inserted the chief.

"Neither of the Martins ever gave a key to the building to anyone and he still has both of his keys to the building." David informed him. The chief thought for a moment and then decided that Harry Sessions should be brought in for questioning.

David and another officer got into a police cruiser and headed for Sims and Sims. When they got there they parked the cruiser and walked into the plumbing company. David showed his badge to the receptionist and asked to see Harry Sessions.

"What's the matter detective?" asked the receptionist.

"Just get Mr. Sessions for us please." answered David. The receptionist paged Harry Sessions while the detectives waited. David remembered when he was here before he had not met Harry because he was out but he had met Don and he had seemed like an okay guy. I wonder if he knows anything about this key business. David thought.

"Detectives" said Harry Sessions as he approached them, "What can I do for you?"

"You can answer a few questions." replied David.

"All right, I'll be glad to, if I can."

"Why are your fingerprints on a key to the Park Hills Condominiums?" asked David.

"I didn't know they were." answered Harry.

"Well, they are and why?" continued David.

"I guess one of our customers must have let me have a key to go out to my truck or to the garage so I wouldn't need to have someone go with me to let me back into the building."

"Who would do that, it's against condo regulations?" prodded David.

"I don't know, but it's the only explanation I can think of ," replied Harry.

"You and Don have done work for the Martins, did Mrs. Martin ever give you a key so you could get back into the building, say when you and Don put in that hot water tank a few weeks ago?" questioned David.

"I don't remember." answered Harry.

"Let's get Don, maybe he will remember if you had to go to the garage ." countered David.

"Oh, yes, I remember, Mrs. Martin gave me her key, we were missing a piece of pipe for the hot water tank. It was on the truck so I went after it but I gave the key back to her as soon as I returned to her condo." related Harry.

"Mr. Martin has his original two keys that he was given when he moved there and so do all the other owners in the building. Where did this 'odd' key with your fingerprints come from?" demanded David.

"I don't know." said Harry "I want a lawyer."

"Come with us to the station now and you can call a lawyer from there." answered David.

They arrived at the station and David took Harry back to the interrogation room. "Your fingerprints were found on a key to the Park Hills Condominiums and the key was found just outside the Martin's condo. How did it get there and how did your fingerprints get on it?" demanded David.

"I don't know and I want to see a lawyer." answered Harry.

"Your lawyer's been called, he's on his way, all you have to do is tell me why your prints are on this key and you can go home." David told him.

"I've told you that I don't know and I'm not saying anymore until my lawyer gets here."

"It doesn't look good, Harry, to have your prints on a key that's been found at a murder scene and that key opens the door to the building, what were you doing with it?"

"I didn't have that key!"

"Then why are your prints on it?" The door opened and a large man filled the doorway.

"Why detective are you questioning my client without council present?"

"I only have one simple question." answered David, "How did his prints get on a key that was found outside the door of a murder scene?"

"You brought him down town for that? Are you charging him with anything?" asked the attorney.

"No, not for now." answered David.

"Then lets go Mr. Sessions."

After that exchange the attorney and Sessions left. David went to the chief's office.

"Any answers?" asked the chief.

"No, I didn't get anywhere, but I know he had something to do with the murder and the theft," replied David, "He acted guilty and he demanded a lawyer almost as soon as I asked him a question."

"You and I know how that goes, we'll just have to do some good police work, check with all the places that make keys in town and give them Sessions description. Maybe we'll get lucky." directed Connally.

David called Stuart again and made plans for dinner. He knew that she was dying to know the 'particulars' of the case and where the key fit in. After all if it weren't for her persistence they wouldn't have found the key.

Stuart was anxious to see David for several reasons; where the key would lead them, hopefully to Mr. Waxler's innocence, and then she just wanted to be with David again. She was definitely attracted to him, more so than to any man she had ever known. He was strong, smart, principled, and good-looking with a great sense of humor. She had met and dated lots of men, at home and away from home, but never anyone like David. Her intercom sounded interrupting her thoughts, Mr. Dobbs was calling her to his office. She walked across the hall and into his office speaking briefly to his secretary. He and Sam Dixon were conferring about the case, she couldn't tell them about the discovery of the key, the police had the means to discover whose prints they were and the law firm didn't. Sam Dixon was still studying the 'reasonable doubt' angle and was excited about Stuart's discovery of Mrs. Martin's inheritance. Dobbs felt hopeful as well, but they both agreed that they needed more evidence to prove his innocence. Stuart still didn't tell them about the key and disliked holding anything back from the attorneys. She thought that the key was even more reason to be hopeful. They would be told soon but the police had to be given time to connect the key to the plumber and the plumber to the murder.

Stuart parked her car in the garage and pushed the button for the elevator. The shiny brass doors opened and there stood Jenny.

"Quick, tell me about the key, I could hardly wait for you to get home."

"I'll know more tonight, David is taking me to dinner and by the way, why didn't you tell me the key was a key!"

"And spoil your fun investigating with your detective? I knew you'd find it from my clue, you're like a dog with a bone, you never give up."

"All I'm going to tell you is that the fingerprints on the key belong to one of the plumbers who installed a hot water tank for the Martins. You'll just have to wait until later for more info."

Stuart got off on ten and opened the door to her condo. Taking off her coat she began to think about what she would wear tonight, she wanted to look really good at dinner and began looking through her wardrobe. She decided on a Camel colored wool pants suit and a white silk blouse that she wore open at the throat. With this she wore a single strand of gold beads and her earrings, large gold hoops. Just then the buzzer sounded, he was here.

CHAPTER 19

Harry Sessions went home and not back to work. He told his attorney nothing except that he didn't know how his fingerprints got on the key. That wasn't true of course, he remembered too well how his prints got on that key.

A plan had begun to form in his mind when he overheard Mrs. Martin talking to her Insurance Agent, if he had those coins he could pay off his bookie.

Mrs. Martin often gave him the key to the inside garage door so he could get to his truck outside the garage. This key opened all the outside doors leading into the building as well. The outside garage door was opened by pushing a button. Harry knew it would be easy to make an impression of this key.

The next time he had needed to go to his truck for some tools Mrs. Martin had given him the key like she always had, she trusted him and Don. He had waited until he was inside the truck before he pressed both sides of the key into alginate (a wax like mineral) making an impression of the key. That had taken all of a minute. He was back to the Martin's condo shortly and returned the key to Mrs. Martin. He took the impressions home with him and that night filled the impressions with acrylic powder mixed with water. In a couple of hours he had two sides of an acrylic key. to the building. Then he glued the two sides together with epoxy and it was strong enough to open the door. He brushed it lightly with brass paint so that it looked like a real key. It would look strange if someone happened to see him with an acrylic key. Now all he had to do was wait.

Harry didn't have to wait too long. The Martins were going away for a long weekend while Mr. Martin attended a seminar. That was the perfect time for him to steal the coins. The best time to break in was on Sunday night, the Martin's weren't due back until Tuesday. So he got into the building with no problem and into the Martin's condo with no problem. He found the coins and was on his way out when Mrs. Martin appeared. He hadn't planned on killing anyone but he had no choice, he had to have those coins! His bookie's boss would kill him if he didn't pay his debt. After he had killed Mrs. Martin he hid behind a fake tree in the corridor, that must have been when the key had fallen out of his pants pocket, too late he had remembered that his pocket had a hole in it. He never knew where the key had fallen until now, he had thought he was 'home free'. Of course it was Mrs. Martin's fault, the whole thing. She shouldn't have come home early, she shouldn't have let anyone use her key and she shouldn't have died but Harry was sure glad he could pay off his bookie. It had been him or her!

CHAPTER 20

Stuart got home early from her date with David because the chief had called him back to headquarters. She pushed the button for the elevator and stood waiting in the lobby. The brass doors opened, she stepped inside and there stood Jenny.

"Now, tell me everything" Jenny blurted out.

"I've already told you that the fingerprints belong to that plumber from Sims and Sims. They brought him in for questioning and he claims to know nothing about why his fingerprints are on the key." related Stuart.

"What are they going to do now?" asked Jenny.

"At dinner David told me that the chief was considering getting a search warrant for the plumber's house."

Jenny frowned as she said "Don't they think it's a little late to be finding the coins, surely he must have gotten rid of them by now."

"The coins aren't the only thing the police are looking for, there's the murder weapon that's missing, too." answered Stuart..

"I should know that the police have all the bases covered." said Jenny and then she asked "Do the police think they've got enough evidence against Harry Sessions to make a case?"

"If the police want a search warrant then I would assume they think he's a good suspect for the murder and the theft." The elevator came to a stop on the tenth floor and as Stuart got off she said, "See you later, Jenny, as soon as I know anything more I'll let you know." The doors closed and the elevator was gone again.

Stuart took off her coat and put away her pocketbook and turned on the CD player. She was so drawn to love songs lately, this time it was Buble singing "Night and Day". She was thinking about David and how a murder had brought them together, they likely would not have met otherwise. Fate had thrown them together and where and how would it all end? She needed to talk to her family about how important David had become in her life. She could just hear her brother Johnny "Here we go again folks, fasten your seatbelts!" He was such a tease and she missed him a lot, they had always been close. She felt that he and David would get along great, they had chosen different careers but both were smart, principled and had good senses of humor. Pretty soon she drifted off to sleep still thinking about David.

After David had taken Stuart home he drove back to the police station. Chief Connally was in his office waiting for David. "What's up chief?"

"I'm getting a search warrant for Sessions' place and I wanted to talk to you before you go." explained Connally.

"I'm sure that he's gotten rid of the coins by now," reasoned David, "but we might find something else to tie him to the murder."

"We need to find anything, I'm certain he had a lot to do with the murder." answered the chief.

"I'm beginning to feel like Stuart, John Waxler was too smart to have lost a key to the building and he didn't need to steal one since all the keys were already in his office," added David, "and he would have had an alibi already in place."

"While you're searching Sessions' place find out if he's left handed." directed Connally.

David and a couple of police officers left on their mission. They arrived at Sessions and rang the doorbell, Sessions opened the door looking more than a little surprised. "What do you fellas want, you've already had me at the station?"

"We have a search warrant for your house." replied David.

"I'm calling my lawyer, you can't do this!"

"Read the warrant sir, we can do this." answered David. The three men stepped into the house and began their search. David walked into the kitchen to look around and spied Session's tool bag on the counter. All of a sudden this triggered his memory of the murder........ killed by blunt force trauma, any of those tools could be used as a murder weapon. He opened the bag and looked at the contents, typical plumbing tools. He called to Sessions "These all your tools?"

"Yes." answered Session "Anything else we need is furnished by Sims and Sims."

David allowed the other policemen time to check the house while he checked the garage. When they were finished David picked up the tool bag and started out of the house.

"Hey, where are you going with my tools, I have to work in the morning!" screamed Session.

"You may have them back tomorrow afternoon but as for in the morning, you'll have to use the company's tools," answered David "and by the way are you right handed or left handed?"

"I'm left handed as you will see by some of my tools and Sims and Sims don't have tools for lefties so I need my tools back."

"You'll get them back tomorrow afternoon."

The three policemen drove back to the station discussing the case. None of them had found anything except David. If Sessions had stolen the coins they were long gone now. The other two policemen questioned David about the tool bag. "I'm going to test all the tools for blood," explained David "they're all blunt instruments that could have been used as a murder weapon."

The chief was waiting when they returned, "Well, what did you find?"

"We found nothing to do with the coins but we just may have found the murder weapon, we'll have to test it and see." answered David. The four of them went back to the Lab and asked CSI to test the entire contents of the tool bag for blood. The CSI doing the testing took out the largest tools ------ tools capable of killing someone. The two most likely were the wrench and the hammer. The CSI took a photograph of each and then put on rubber gloves and a white Lab coat. He got a sterile cotton swab dipped it in distilled water, and then he swabbed small spots on different places on the wrench. Before going further he drew a diagram of the wrench and marked the places where he had swabbed the water. He had swabbed the most likely places for blood to be found. After swabbing the wrench the CSI used a blue light on it and the blood showed up. After this happened he went back outside the Lab and reported to Chief Connally that indeed blood had been found on the wrench.

"At last a lead!" exclaimed David.

"That key is becoming the turning point in this investigation," said the chief, "thank Miss Browning for us."

The CSI broke into the conversation, "You realize that now blood has been found on the wrench it must be matched to Mrs. Martin?"

"How long will that take?" asked David.

"Marshall University's Forensic Lab is backed up but I think we'll have it in a week." answered the CSI.

"What about the State Police Lab in Charleston?" questioned David.

"Same song, same words, they're backed up, too." replied the CSI.

"Then it will be about a week before we know whether the blood matches Mrs. Martin?"

"Yes." responded the CSI.

"Let's just hope that the murderer doesn't get away before we can arrest him!" said the chief.

"He wants his tools back tomorrow and I told him I'd get them back tomorrow afternoon," interjected David.

"Has anyone got an old wrench at home that could pass for this one?" asked Connally. "How about we all bring a wrench to work tomorrow and see if we have a match?"

In David's mind Harry Sessions was the killer and the DNA from the wrench would prove it. What would he tell Stuart? What *COULD* he tell Stuart? She deserved an answer of some kind since she had found the key but how much should she be told? He would have to wrestle with that answer.

CHAPTER 21

Stuart awoke and wondered why David hadn't called her last evening to tell her what was going on. Did they get a search warrant for Sessions' home? Did they find anything? Her life had certainly changed since she had moved to Huntington. She had never been involved with murder before, much less helping to catch a murderer and holding conversations with a ghost? When she had walked thru this doorway she had found more than she bargained for. It was all pretty exciting, though, even if her friends and family could never have pictured her right in the middle of a murder case.

She got ready for work and after eating her breakfast she left her condo and rang for the elevator. When she got to work she had a hard time not disclosing to the attorneys her discovery of the key. But she had to wait on the police department since they were the only ones who could 'connect the dots'. David called her soon after she arrived at the office. "Can you get away for lunch today?"

"You bet I can but don't know if I can wait until lunch to hear the news."

"Meet me at the Café at noon."

"See you then." Stuart answered and hung up the phone.

In the meantime David had to think about what he could tell Stuart and how much he could tell her.

Stuart left to meet David at the Café. She got there first so she had the hostess show her to a booth. While she waited for David she drummed her finger tips on the table, she was really anxious to hear the news. David walked in the Café and the hostess directed him to Stuart.

"You look pretty as always, Stuart." said David as he sat down.

"Thank you, flattery will get you everywhere but about your news?"

"Let's order first and then we'll talk" David said as he motioned to the waitress. They made good hamburgers at the Café so they both ordered hamburgers and french fries with coffee later.

"I must caution you again, none of this can be told to your attorneys yet." began David "We got a warrant to search Sessions' house, the chief found a judge to issue the warrant.. We didn't find anything until I saw his plumber's tool bag and realized it could hold several 'blunt instruments'. I took it with me and promised to return it this afternoon. He demanded I return it last night so he could take it to work this morning."

"Can you do that?" questioned Stuart.

"Sure, we're looking for the murder weapon and a plumber's tool bag is full of tools that could be used as 'blunt instruments'. We took the bag back to headquarters and gave it to CSI to test for blood and there on the wrench was blood."

"Oh, I just knew Mr. Waxler couldn't have committed murder." exclaimed Stuart. "Now where does this leave Martin and his girlfriend?"

"Still playing house across the river." replied David "but if the blood on the wrench matches Mrs. Martin's DNA then Waxler will be released."

"Then Mr. Martin didn't have anything to do with his wife's murder?"

"I didn't say that," continued David. "as I told you before, he could have paid someone to do it."

"How long before we'll know if the blood is Mrs. Martin's?" asked Stuart.

"About a week." replied David "I hope no longer than that. The Forensics labs are backed up."

"Oh, how I wish I could tell Mr. Waxler." said Stuart.

"Well, it won't be long now before Waxler is released." replied David "I just hope Sessions doesn't skip town before we know about the blood."

Their lunch arrived and while they were eating David told Stuart that Chief Connally had asked him to convey his gratitude to her for helping them with the case.

"I thought you promised not to tell the chief about me, I was supposed to be an anonymous informer!"

"You can hardly be anonymous when you find a key right outside the door of a murder scene, in your condo building. You can tell your attorneys as soon as we can pick up Sessions for murder. You can explain that we wouldn't let you tell them because it was an ongoing murder investigation."

They finished lunch and Stuart went back to the office and David went back to police headquarters after promising to call Stuart the minute he knew anything.

The chief had brought his wrench to the station as had the other detectives including David. The only wrench that looked old and used was Connally's, it matched Sessions' almost perfectly. He called David to his office and they traded Connally's wrench for Sessions' and David left to return the tool bag. He drove to Sims and Sims but left the tool bag in the car while he went to find Sessions. He called him aside and told him the tool bag was in the car, "I didn't want your boss to know we had taken your tool bag, it might be hard for you to explain, come with me to the car and get it."

"Thanks a lot,. you shouldn't have taken it in the first place." answered Sessions sarcastically.

"Well you've got it back now, sorry to inconvenience you." replied David. At least Sessions hadn't seemed suspicious that we might have found anything of importance, thought David as he drove back to the station. He went straight to the chief's office to report on Sessions and the tool bag. Connally had already sent Sessions' wrench to the Forensic lab and had been told it would be at least a week before they could test for DNA.

"How did Sessions react to getting his tool bag back?" asked the chief.

"He was still mad but glad to get it back, I acted as if it were standard police procedure and was sorry to have bothered him."

"And he believed you?"

"Yes, I think he did, he probably thought that I would have arrested him if anything had shown up." answered David.

"Well, now we play a waiting game." added Connally.

CHAPTER 22

Stuart could hardly wait to get home and tell Jenny the news but Mr. Dobbs called Stuart to his office to have a meeting about strategy for the case. Thus far the best defense they had for Waxler was reasonable doubt. They discussed this point again and thought they could make a good case against Martin, at least as good as the police had against Waxler, after all inheriting $1,000,000 at Mrs. Martin's death was $990,000 more reasons than the $10,000 the coins would bring.

As they discussed witnesses, testimonies, etc., Stuart was becoming more embarrassed about her secret. The attorneys were working so hard. Finally they finished their meeting and Stuart saw that it was almost five o'clock. She said goodnight to the attorneys and went to her office to pick up her bag and left.

She parked in the garage and rushed to the elevator hoping to find Jenny. The shiny doors opened and there stood Jenny. "I'm so glad to see you." Stuart said excitedly, "I have lots to tell you."

"Can it wait?" asked Jenny, "Meet me on the elevator at six thirty."

"See you at six thirty." promised Stuart as she got off on the tenth floor. She laughed to herself as she thought, who would ever believe that she had a date at six thirty with a ghost on an elevator. She was in a good mood after having lunch with David and was looking forward to telling Jenny the good news.

At exactly six thirty Stuart stepped out of her condo and pushed the button for the elevator. The elevator made its way to the tenth floor, the doors opened and there stood Jenny. "Get in" said Jenny "I want to hear everything."

"Why did you want me to wait until six thirty?" questioned Stuart.

"Because the elevator is busy between five and six thirty."

"Duh, don't know why I didn't think of that," replied Stuart "Well, David found the murder weapon at Sessions' house, at least he's almost sure that it is, and it has now been sent to the Forensic Lab for DNA testing. Blood was found on a wrench in Sessions' tool bag so they are now trying to match it to Mrs. Martin. This will take about a week."

"That means the case is almost solved?" asked Jenny.

"Yes." replied Stuart "and you played the biggest part in solving it. Wish I could tell Mr. Waxler and David and of course the attorneys."

"How soon would they release Mr. Waxler if Mrs. Martin's DNA is found on the wrench?"

"Oh right away, I'm sure." answered Stuart.

"When's your next date with Detective Moore?"

Stuart smiled as she answered, "I don't know but he promised to call me the moment he heard from the Lab and by the way how is your search coming? any answers yet?"

"Yes, I'm close to getting what I came here to get and I believe your detective is interested in more than just solving a murder with you," said Jenny as she changed the subject.

"I certainly hope so!" said Stuart and they both laughed. The elevator came back to the tenth floor and Stuart got off saying good night to Jenny.

Stuart put on her pajamas after a warm shower and sat down to listen to another song by Buble. Again one of Sinatra's best, "Just In Time"; had she and David met 'just in time'?......time would tell.

David made his way to Chief Connally's office after stopping at the CSI lab to ask if they had heard anything from Sessions' wrench. He knocked on the chief's door and Connally told him to come in.

"Have you been able to find any connection between Sessions and Martin?" the Chief asked.

"No sir, with the exception of Sessions doing plumbing work for the Martins," replied David "but my sources tell me that Sessions is into gambling big time."

"With the wrong people?" questioned Connally "Definitely the wrong people, often gets in over his head as most gamblers do." answered David.

"Then that could be his motive for killing Mrs. Martin and stealing the coins."

"We won't be able to trace the coins but I don't think the prosecutor will have any trouble getting a conviction with Mrs. Martin's DNA on Sessions' wrench." offered David.

"Well, we won't have to wait much longer, the report should be here in another couple of days." Connally informed him.

CHAPTER 23

Stuart was getting dressed for work when her phone rang. It was David with good news. "The DNA report is back and it is Mrs. Martin's blood on Sessions wrench."

"Wonderful, now can I tell my attorneys about my part in all of this?" asked Stuart.

"Sure, go right ahead but I suspect they will already know about the DNA report by the time you get to work. But I will back you up on why you couldn't tell them before."

Stuart could hardly wait to get to the office. She dressed hurriedly and dashed out of her condo. The elevator doors opened and there stood Jenny. "I'm so glad you're here." said Stuart.

"Has the report come back?" asked Jenny.

"Yes and it is Mrs. Martin's DNA on the wrench and they are going to pick up Sessions right away." continued Stuart.

"At last," sighed Jenny, "how does David feel about your sleuthing ability?"

"I'll forgive you for not telling me the key was a real key, now that the key has caught Sessions. Of course you know we couldn't have found it without you and that key might not have been found for a long time, we all owe you a lot. I just wish I could tell David and Mr. Waxler. Oh, I keep forgetting to ask you how you knew that Sessions first name was Harry?"

"You must have mentioned it someplace along the way, Oops, somebody wants the elevator, I'm so glad that everything is turning out okay for Mr. Waxler and that Sessions is going to get what's coming to him, it's been a blast working with you." said Jenny as she started the elevator again.

"Now we'll have to get to work on your answers, I'd better get to work too, so see you later." answered Stuart. She got off in the garage and got into her car. By the time she arrived at her office she was calmer, she opened the office door and was greeted by Sam Dixon "John Waxler is being released today, the police have found the real murderer and Chief Connally said you could fill us in on the rest."

"I hated not being able to tell you what I had discovered but the police wouldn't allow it because it was an ongoing murder investigation." and then she told them the rest of the story.

"That was smart of you to call the police after finding that key and then not touching it until the detective arrived." said Robert Dobbs.

"Thank you, keeping it from you was one of the hardest things I've ever had to do." replied Stuart.

"Reasonable doubt can be kind of tricky, if that's all you have at trial. We're oh so glad you found that key!" offered Sam Dixon.

Stuart felt a lot better after listening to the attorneys. She was so afraid she had overstepped some boundaries investigating this case and not able to tell the attorneys about her discoveries. But they seemed genuinely pleased with her 'snooping'.

Before lunch Stuart's phone rang and it was David "How about celebrating with dinner at "21" in the Frederick building?"

"I'd love it!' exclaimed Stuart "Pick me up at seven thirty.

"You got it, see you then." The Frederick building was directly across Fourth Avenue from the Keith Albee Performing Arts Center. It was once the leading hotel in the western half of West Virginia and at least fifty years older than the Keith Albee, now it housed a great restaurant and various business offices but still held on to its former splendor.

Everything was coming together, Mr. Waxler was getting out of jail and the real murderer was getting in. Stuart wished she could tell everyone about Jenny and how she was responsible for all of it but that was out of the question and it would have to stay that way.

David and a couple of other policemen went to pick up Sessions. He was taken by surprise and at first refused to go but David handcuffed him and arrested him for murder. By the time they arrived at the station the sweat was trickling down his face. He asked for an attorney so one was called and then they led him back to the interrogation room. "I haven't done anything, what are you doing?"

"You've done a lot Harry and we're going to see that you pay for it!" announced David "We not only have the key to the condo building with your prints on it but we have the murder weapon, found in your tool bag, with Mrs. Martin's DNA."

"I didn't mean to do it! She was supposed to be out of town, I only wanted the coins, I owed my bookie a lot of money and those coins were my only way out, they would've killed me if I hadn't paid up." Sessions said as his voice trailed off.

"We knew about your gambling addiction, guess it finally caught up with you," replied David as he called a policeman to take Sessions to a cell.

Stuart thought the condo association should have a Welcome Home party for John even if it were on short notice. She called the condo association president and they made plans to have the party in the condo meeting room. Stuart thought by five o'clock John Waxler should be released and home. The rest of the Board thought the party was a great idea so the plans were set for five o'clock.

As Stuart drove home from work early she put the party on the back burner and began to think about what she would wear to dinner. She wanted to dress up, not just wear a pants suit but not too fancy either. She parked the car in the garage and walked to the elevator, she pushed the button and the doors opened but no Jenny. She hadn't often seen Jenny twice in one day so she didn't really expect to see her. The elevator stopped on her floor and she got off. She went directly to the closet to find something to wear to dinner and decided on a little black dress with long sleeves and a wide V-neckline. She selected a long double strand of pearls and pearl drop earrings.

There was no time to change before the party it was almost five o'clock. She left her condo and took the elevator to the lobby. Almost all the owners were present and waiting in the meeting room. The president of the association had gone to get Waxler and they should be here soon. Everyone was excited. At about ten minutes past five they heard the elevator stop in the lobby and almost immediately the door to the meeting room opened and they all yelled "Welcome Home!"

John Waxler stood frozen in the doorway but smiling from ear to ear. "Thank You," he said, "it's wonderful to be home!" Everyone gathered around him to tell him how glad they were that his ordeal was over and that they had never believed he was a murderer. There was a popping noise and everyone turned to see Bob Hancock and Hank Symes pouring champagne into glasses. When they all had their glasses they saluted John Waxler and wished him well.

Stuart stayed to add her congratulations when Waxler walked to the middle of the room and asked for silence, "I want all of you to know that without Miss Browning's help I would still be in jail and it was her discovery that solved the case!" Stuart flushed as she received a large round of applause. Then they all wanted to know what she discovered and how she found it. She gave them the short version without mentioning Jenny. She had been looking around on the sixth floor when she saw a key. She then called the police and the key was taken to police headquarters. They found fingerprints matching a plumber who had recently done some work for the Martins. With some good police work they had picked up the real murderer and he was now in jail.

"When you called the police was it that good-looking detective that you called?" asked one of the women.

"Why, yes it was." answered Stuart.

"You two make a handsome couple." continued the woman.

"Thank you." said Stuart flushing again. She finally got away and went up to her condo. No Jenny this time either.

Stuart went directly to her bedroom and started to get ready for her date. She took a shower and then laid out her clothes. She began with sheer black hose and black open toed shoes with very high heels. Her black dress slipped easily over her head and she fastened it with a short zipper in the back. The double strand of long pearls looked great with this dress. She combed her long blond hair and put on the pearl drop earrings. With her fair coloring she looked stunning in black. She wore a bit more blush on her cheeks and a little deeper shade of pink lipstick. She got out her black purse and filled it with all the things that women carry in their purses. The buzzer sounded and Stuart pushed the button to let David in. She slipped on her black cashmere coat and picked up her purse, opened her door and then locked it and stood waiting for the elevator doors to open. Out stepped David looking surprised that she had on her coat and had locked her condo door. "I could have met you downstairs but I didn't think in time." explained Stuart.

"That's all right, I always enjoy the anticipation of waiting to see you while I ride the elevator." They took the elevator back to the lobby and walked outside where David's car was parked close to the front door.

They arrived at "21" at about seven forty-five and the hostess showed them to a table on the far side of the room, in the corner. When the waitress arrived they gave her their drink orders. As they sat waiting David said, "You make a good detective Miss Browning, the police department thanks you and I thank you, now are you going to tell me who your mysterious friend is who gave you those clues?"

"No, I've already told you that I promised not to." replied Stuart.

"But I thought that now the case was over this phantom wouldn't mind your telling me who she is."

"No, that will have to remain a secret forever besides you'd never believe it anyway."

"Has Mr. Waxler been released yet?"

"Yes, we had a Welcome Home party for him."

"That was nice." said David. "Are you really not going to tell me?"

"Do you believe in ghosts?"

"Of course not!"

"I didn't think so," Their wine arrived and they toasted their victory. David looked at Stuart in her black dress and long pearls with her blond hair falling over one shoulder and thought that he had never seen her look lovelier and forgot all about the mysterious friend.

After dinner while they drank their coffee David asked, "Now that the case is over do you think you'll get another exciting one?"

"Well I certainly hope not *THIS* exciting!" answered Stuart, "what will you be working on?"

"I'm thinking of going to law school, would you be my paralegal when I get through?" teased David.

"But of course!" laughed Stuart "We work so well together." David gazed at the beautiful young woman before him and almost without thinking the words came tumbling out "Will we get married before or after law school?"

Stuart looked to see if he were teasing and saw that he was completely serious and it took her breath away. Was he really asking her to marry him? It was a minute or two before she could answer. She looked at him with love in her eyes and replied, "I vote for *BEFORE* law school!"

"Let's get out of here." whispered David.

As they walked to the car David put his arm around Stuart. Once inside the car David asked, "Did you really say *yes* back there?"

"Stop talking and kiss me." replied Stuart.

"I love you." said David as he kissed her.

CHAPTER 24

It had been several days since Stuart had seen Jenny and she was anxious to tell her about David's proposal and the party for Mr. Waxler. Jenny was always disappearing, where did she go? She could be so annoying but she had been so helpful in solving the murder, Stuart guessed that she would just have to wait on Jenny's timetable.

Stuart returned to the office and began work on a new case with Mr. Dobbs. She took some depositions but her mind wasn't on her work, she was too excited to work, she had talked to her parents and she and David were going to North Carolina on the weekend.

The day seemed endless and Stuart was anxious to check on Jenny again, ghosts could take care of themselves couldn't they? She had become very fond of her and missed their short visits in the elevator. Finally the day ended and Stuart left her office, all the way home she kept trying to convince herself that Jenny would be there this time.

After parking her car in the garage Stuart walked to the elevator hoping Jenny would appear. Those shiny brass doors opened but Jenny wasn't there, she rode all the way to the tenth floor and no Jenny. She turned around as she was getting off the elevator and saw something in the back right corner. She pressed the button to hold the elevator door open and then stepped back inside and picked up the leather strap with the pewter peace symbol hanging on it, then she knew Jenny's mission was finished. But she began to wonder… did Harry Sessions?…No, of course not.

"I shall miss you Jenny and your key that opened more than a door." whispered Stuart. And speaking of doors she could hardly wait to open the next door where David was waiting. Would she ever tell him about Jenny?…… Maybe in twenty or thirty years !